ELIZABETH

Angel Creek Christmas Brides, Book #8

JO GRAFFORD

ISBN: 978-1-944794-41-5

About this Series

After the war leaves Charleston devastated, and with little prospects of marriage, five friends head west for a new life and a possible love match. A year later, they're homesick and in desperate need for a deeper connection with their old life so what else would a Southern Belle do other than invite more friends to join them?

Angel Creek is about to be invaded by six new Southern Misses and the town may never be the same again!

CHRISTMAS 2018 BOOKS

Book 1: Charity — Sylvia McDaniel
Book 2: Julia — Lily Graison
Book 3: Ruby — Hildie McQueen
Book 4: Sarah — Peggy McKenzie
Book 5: Anna — Everly West

CHRISTMAS 2019 BOOKS

Book 6: Caroline — Lily Graison
Book 7: Melody — Caroline Clemmons
Book 8: Elizabeth — Jo Grafford
Book 9: Emma — Peggy McKenzie
Book 10: Viola — Cyndi Raye
Book 11: Ginger — Sylvia McDaniel

Introduction

C *an the hope and joy of Christmas light the way for two hearts devastated by war?*

Elizabeth Byrd receives an invitation to join her friends in Angel Creek, Montana to become a mail-order bride. At first, the young combat nurse is scandalized by the idea of agreeing to marry a man she's never met, but the war has taken everything from her — her brothers, too many friends to count, and her fiancé. There's nothing left for her in Charleston but more heartache.

Captain David Pemberton retreats to his hunting lodge in Montana the moment the war is over. He's looking forward to being alone with the memories of his wife who passed in the early days of the fighting. But the men of Angel Creek don't see fit to leave a widowed soldier alone during Christmas. Insisting four years is long enough to grieve, they dare him to join them on a holiday venture to acquire wives for them all — a dare he accepts in a weak moment.

He receives the shock of his life at who steps off the train to claim his hand in marriage.

Whispers In Wyoming

A Multi-Author Series

His Wish, Her Command

His Heart, Her Love

Other Multi-Author Series Books

Holliday Islands Resort — The Dashing Groom

Silverpines Series #27 —Wanted: Bounty Hunter

Silverpines Companion Tale —The Bounty Hunter's Sister

The Bride Herder — Herd the Heavens

The Belles of Wyoming — Wild Rose Summer

Brides of Pelican Rapids — Rebecca's Dream

Sailors and Saints — The Sailor and the Surgeon

Her Billionaire Series

written exclusively by Jo Grafford

Her Billionaire Boss

Her Billionaire Bodyguard — *coming soon!*

Lost Colony Series

written exclusively by Jo Grafford

Breaking Ties

Trail of Crosses

Into the Mainland

Higher Tides (Series Finale) — *coming Thanksgiving!*

To receive a personal email each time Jo releases a new book, sign up for her New Release Email at www.JoGrafford.com or follow her on Bookbub at www.bookbub.com/authors/jo-grafford for an instant but shorter announcement.

Acknowledgments

Thank you beaucoup to Trudy Cordle, Jhommie Giorla Kem-ing, Marcia Montoya, and Amy Petrowich for beta reading this story. I also want to give a shout-out to my Cuppa Jo Readers on Facebook for reading and loving my books!

New readers are always welcome to join us at https://www.facebook.com/groups/CuppaJoReaders for book chats, behind-the-scenes peeks, parties, cover reveals, giveaways, and more!

Much love, Jo

Chapter 1: Cautious Arrival

ELIZABETH

Early November, 1866

E lizabeth Byrd rubbed icy hands up and down her arms beneath her threadbare navy wool cloak as she gingerly hopped down from the stagecoach. It was so much colder in Montana than it had been in South Carolina. She gazed around her at the hard-packed earthen streets, scored by the ruts of many wagon wheels. They probably would have been soft and muddy if it weren't for the brisk winds swirling above them. Instead, they were stiff with cold and covered in a layer of frost that glinted like rosy crystals beneath the setting sun.

Plain, saltbox buildings of weathered gray planks hovered over the streets like watchful sentinels, as faded and tattered as the handful of citizens scurrying past — women in faded gingham dresses and bonnets along with a half-dozen or so men in work clothes and dusty top hats. More than likely, they were in a hurry to get home, since it was fast approaching the dinner hour. Her stomach rumbled out a contentious reminder at how long it had been since her own last meal.

So this was Angel Creek.

At least I'll fit in. She glanced ruefully down at her workaday brown dress and the scuffed toes of her boots. Perhaps, wearing the castoffs of her former maid, Lucy, wasn't the most brilliant idea she'd ever come up with. However, it was the only plan she'd been able to conjure up on such short notice. A young woman traveling alone couldn't be too careful these days. For her own safety, she'd wanted to attract as little attention as possible during her long journey west. It had worked. Few folks had given her more than a cursory glance the entire trip, leaving her plenty of time to silently berate herself for accepting the challenge of her dear friend, Caroline, to change her stars by becoming a mail-order bride like a few of their friends had done the year before.

"Thanks to the war, there's nothing left for us here in Charleston, love. You know it, and I know it," Caroline had chided gently. Then she'd leaned in to embrace her tenderly. "I know you miss him. We all do." She was referring to Elizabeth's fiancé who'd perished in battle. "But he would want you to go on and keep living. That means dusting off your broken heart and finding a man to marry while you're still young enough to have a family of your own."

She and her friends were in their early twenties, practically rusticating on the shelf in the eyes of those who'd once comprised the social elite in Charleston. They were confirmed spinsters now, yesterday's news, has-beens…

"However, there are still scads of marriageable men lined up and waiting for us in Angel Creek." They'd discovered this marvelous fact by an ad placed in The Groom's Gazette. "Every one of our friends who traveled

9

there last year are happily married and very anxious for us to join them. All you have to do is pack your things and get on the train with us."

And leave behind everyone and everything I've ever known. Elizabeth shivered, pulled her cloak more tightly around her, and attempted to duck her chin farther down inside the collar, wondering if she'd just made the biggest mistake of her life. She was in Angel Creek days later than most of her friends had agreed on, having wrestled like the dickens with her better judgment to make up her mind to join them.

There were six of them this year — Caroline, Melody, Emma, Viola, Ginger and herself. All were former debutantes from Charleston, just like the five brides who'd begun this outlandish venture the previous Christmas. All were from impoverished families whose properties and bank accounts had been devastated by the war. It was the only reason she'd been willing to even consider such a foolish idea. She was fast running out of options. Her widowed mother was barely keeping food on the table for her three younger sisters.

Even so, it had been a last-minute decision, one she'd made too late to begin any correspondence with her intended groom. She didn't even know the man's name, only that he would be waiting for her in Angel Creek when her stagecoach rolled into town. Or so Caroline had promised. Her friend had arrived days ago and was likely already married now.

With a sigh of resignation, Elizabeth reached down to grasp the handles of her two travel bags that the stage driver had unloaded for her. The rest of her belongings would arrive in the coming days. There'd been too many trunks to bring along by stage. In the meantime, she hoped and prayed she was doing the right thing for her loved ones. At worst, her reluctant decision to leave home meant one less mouth for her mama to feed. At best, she might claw her way back to some modicum of social significance and be in the position to help her family in some way. Some day...

Her hopes in that regard plummeted the second she laid eyes on the two men in the wagon rumbling in her direction. It was a rickety vehicle with no overhead covering. It creaked and groaned with each turn of its wheels, a problem that might have easily been solved with a squirt of oil. Then again, the heavily patched trousers of both men indicated they were as poor as church mice. More than likely, they didn't possess any extra coin for oil.

Of all the rotten luck! She bit her lower lip. *I'm about to marry a man as poor as myself.* So much for her hopes of improving her lot in life enough to send money home to Mama and the girls!

The driver slowed his team, a pair of red-brown geldings. They were much lovelier than the rattle-trap they were pulling. "Elizabeth Byrd, I presume?" he inquired in a rich baritone that was neither unpleasant nor overly warm and welcoming.

Her insides froze to a block of ice. This time, it wasn't because of the frigid northern temperatures. She recognized that face, that voice; and with them, came a flood of heart wrenching emotions.

"You!" she exclaimed. Her travel bags slid from her nerveless fingers to the ground once more. A hand flew to her heart, as she relived the sickening dread all over again that she'd experienced at the Battle of James Island. She was the unlucky nurse who'd delivered the message to Captain David Pemberton that his wife had passed during childbirth. The babe hadn't survived, either. But what, in heaven's name, was the tragic officer doing so far from home? Unless she was mistaken, his family was from the Ft. Sumpter area.

"Nurse Byrd." The captain handed his reins to the man sitting next to him, a grizzled older fellow who was dressed in a well-pressed brown suit, though both knees bore patches. "We meet again." He offered her a two-fingered salute and reached for her travel bags. He was even more handsome than she remembered, despite the well-worn Stetson shading his piercing bourbon eyes. During their last encounter, he'd been clean shaven. His light brown sideburns now traveled down to a shortly clipped beard. If the offbeat rhythm of her heart was any indication, he wore the more rugged look rather nicely.

Which was neither here nor there. Elizabeth gave herself a mental shake. She'd been searching for a sign, anything that would shed light on whether she was doing the right thing by coming to Angel Creek. Encountering this man, of all people, only a handful of minutes after her arrival, seemed a pretty clear indication of just how horrible a mistake she'd made.

She nudged the handles of her bags with the toe of her boot to put them out of reach. "Y-you don't have to go through with this, captain. I can only imagine how difficult it is for you to lay eyes on me again." If it was anything close to how difficult it was for her to lay eyes on him, it would behoove them both to take off running in opposite directions. "I am quite happy to board with one of my friends until I can secure passage back to South Carolina." The whole trip had been a horrible miscalculation of judgment. She could see that now as she stared stonily into the face of the officer who'd led the man to whom she was once affianced into the battle that had claimed his life. Captain Pemberton didn't know that wretched fact, of course. How could he? They were neither personally, nor closely, acquainted at the time.

The expression in his eyes softened a few degrees as he regarded her. "I gather you found the young man you were searching for during the war?" he noted quietly. "Otherwise, you would not be here."

Preparing to marry you, you mean! "I found him, yes." Her voice was tight with cold and misery. It was all she could do to keep her teeth from chattering. "I found him and buried him."

"Ah." He nodded sadly. "Words are never adequate in situations like these. Nevertheless, I am deeply sorry for your loss."

His regret appeared genuine. She sensed he was a kind man, a good man, despite the deplorable circumstances under which they'd made their first acquaintance. *More's the pity!* Though she couldn't exactly hold the captain responsible for the Union bullet that had taken her Charley's life, she couldn't just up and marry the man responsible for leading him into harm's way, either. Could she?

Perhaps it was the cold breeze numbing her brain, but suddenly she was no longer certain about a good number of things.

"Come, Elizabeth." The commanding note in David Pemberton's voice brooked no further arguments. "You must be famished after such a long journey, and you'll catch your death out here if we linger in the cold."

This time, Elizabeth's toes were too icy to function when he reached for her travel bags. She stood there shivering while he tossed them inside his wagon. She was both shocked and grateful when he proceeded to unbutton his overcoat and slide it around her shoulders.

It was toasty warm from his body heat and smelled

woodsy and masculine. "I th-thank y-you." She was no longer able to hide how badly her teeth were chattering.

"Think nothing of it, Miss Byrd." He slid a protective arm around her shoulders and guided her on down the street. "A friendly fellow named Elijah owns a restaurant next door. Since our wedding isn't for another two hours, how about we head over there for a spell? We can grab a bite to eat and thaw out at the same time."

Our wedding? Her lips parted in protest, but she was shivering too hard to form any words.

As if sensing her confusion, he smiled and leaned closer to speak directly in her ear. His breath warmed her chilly lobe and sent a shot of...something...straight down to her toes. "Surely an angel of mercy like yourself can spare the time to swap a few war stories with an old soldier?"

She clamped her teeth together. *An angel of mercy, indeed!* She'd felt more like an angel of death back there on the battlefield. There were days she lost more soldiers than the ones she managed to save. It was something she preferred never to think of again, much less discuss.

"If I cannot make you smile at least once in the next two hours, I'll purchase your passage back to South Carolina, myself," he teased, tightening his arm around her shoulders.

Now *that* was an offer she couldn't afford to pass up. She didn't currently possess the coin for a return trip, though she had to wonder if the shabbily dressed captain was any better for the funds, himself.

She gave him a tight-lipped nod and allowed him to lead her inside The Eatery.

The tantalizing aromas of fresh-baked bread, hot cider, and some other delectable entrée assailed them, making her mouth water. A pine tree graced one corner of the dining area. Its bows were weighed down with festive gingerbread ornaments and countless strands of red ribbon. A man in a white apron, whom she could only presume was Captain Pemberton's friend, Elijah, cut between a line of tables and hurried in their direction, arms outstretched. "You rebel you! Someone might have at least warned me you were one of the lucky fellers gittin' himself a new wife."

"Oh-h!" Elizabeth's voice came out as a warble of alarm as, from the corner of her eye, she watched a young serving woman heading their way from the opposite direction. She was bearing a tray with a tall cake and holding it in such a manner that she couldn't see over the top of it. She was very much at risk of running in to someone or something.

David Pemberton glanced down at her concern, but all she could do was wave her hand in the direction of the calamity about to take place.

His gaze swiftly followed where she pointed, just in time to watch the unfortunate server and her cake collide with Elijah. White icing and peach preserves flew everywhere. His hair and one side of his face were plastered with a layer of sticky whiteness.

The woman gave a strangled shriek and slid to her knees. A puppy dashed out of nowhere and began to lick the remains of the gooey fluff from her fingers.

Afterwards, Elizabeth would blame it on the long journey for frazzling her nerves to such an extent; because, otherwise, there was no excuse on heaven or earth for what she did next.

She laughed — hysterically! It was ill-mannered of her, unladylike to the extreme, and completely uncalled for, but she couldn't help it. She laughed until there were tears in her eyes.

Captain Pemberton grinned in unholy glee at her. There was such a delicious glint in his whiskey eyes that it made her knees tremble.

"A deal's a deal, nurse; and the way I see it, you did more than smile. You laughed, which means I'll not be needing to purchase that trip back to South Carolina for you, after all. Unless you've any further objections, we've a little less than two hours before we say our vows." He arched one dark brow at her in challenge.

Their gazes clashed, and the world beneath her shifted. As a woman of her word, she suddenly couldn't come up with any more reasons — not a blessed one — why they couldn't or shouldn't get married.

Tonight!

Chapter 2: Wedding Cake

DAVID

David found himself utterly mesmerized by Elizabeth Byrd. Despite her humble dress and cloak, she carried her head and shoulders with the poise of a queen of high society. Well, except when she was nearly doubled over in mirth... And her laugh was so entrancing and so genuine that several patrons in The Eatery kept glancing with curiosity and interest in her direction. And admiration...

He stared down a pair of young chaps a few tables over, treating them to the full blast of his warning glare. She was his wife, or would be shortly. He'd just as soon see them remove their gawking manly eyeballs from her person.

He didn't back down until they lowered their eyes. With a quiet grunt of satisfaction, he returned his attention to his soon-to-be bride. She was fighting to get her outburst of merriment under control.

Elijah, who had disappeared into the kitchen shortly after his collision with the cake, soon came striding back in their direction with a sheepish look on his face. His hair was damp but clear of all traces of the white icing. Plus, he'd changed into a clean shirt and a suit jacket.

"That new server of mine," he grumbled with a grin that countered his gruffness. "She's as nice as all get-out but as clumsy as a whole herd of bulls in a china shop." He produced a white handkerchief and dabbed at a patch of wetness on his neck. "As for your special order, Captain Pemberton…" He darted a quick glance at Elizabeth. "I assure you my, er…staff is hard at work in the kitchen filling that order." He cleared his throat. "It will be delivered to your table shortly." He waved them forward. "I've got a private one set up for you."

That was good news, indeed. David grinned in delight as he placed a hand beneath Elizabeth's elbow and guided her after Elijah. He'd ordered a small but elaborate wedding cake, hoping to impress his affianced. It appeared his hopes, and the fancy price he'd paid for the cake, would not be in vain.

Elizabeth glanced back and forth a few times between him and Elijah, looking puzzled. To her credit, however, she didn't question their host's cryptic message.

No doubt it was her impeccable southern belle manners kicking in. David eyed her threadbare apparel, heart wrenching in pity. Clearly, the Great War hadn't been kind to her or her family. He'd seen and heard stories just like hers all too many times. The southern plantation families had been hit the hardest, many of them devastated in terms of business interests and financial holdings. Clearly, hers been one of those families. The gown she wore was faded and pulling out at the seams in a few places, and — come to think of it — it was a couple sizes too big, as if she'd suddenly dropped weight. A significant amount of it.

The notion that she and her family might not have had enough to eat in recent weeks made his chest hurt.

"Here is your table." Elijah pulled aside a dark curtain to reveal a roughly hewn table for two resting in a windowed alcove. A pair of high-back chairs were canted invitingly in their direction, dressed with cheery red and white checkered cushions. "I'll send someone out right away with a couple of glasses of my fresh squeezed lemonade."

"That sounds delicious." Elizabeth's eyes widened and her lips curved in delight at the matching checkered table-cloth and the flickering candles. "This is so festive and lovely," she sighed.

"Yes. Lovely is exactly the right word." David wondered if she was reminiscing about days gone by, back before the war when things had been easier for her family.

She colored prettily when the double meaning of his words sank him.

As he took his own seat, he found himself unable to remove his gaze from her classically fair features, her elaborate hair style, and the elegant curve of her neck. Elizabeth Byrd might be a former debutante in terms of wardrobe and bank accounts, but she was still every inch a southern belle. She held her head with pride and her shoulders straight, and she moved with the confidence of a woman who knew, or had once known, her proper place in society.

He leaned a few inches in her direction while unfolding and spreading his white linen napkin in his lap. "You must be famished," he noted softly. "I have Elijah's finest pot roast on order, along with his prize winter soup." It was a creamy broth brimming with chicken, vegetables, and hand-kneaded and cut noodles in a variety of holiday shapes — Christmas trees, ornaments, and stars.

"It sounds like a feast," she returned.

"Fitting, don't you think? Considering it is our wedding day." He reached across the table to rest his hand momentarily atop hers. He found her fingers chilled from the outdoors, so he curled his around hers to warm them.

Though her lashes fluttered against her cheeks as if she was startled by the gesture, she left her hand resting beneath his for the space of several heartbeats before gently removing it. "I am accustomed to economizing, Captain Pemberton." She clasped her hands in her lap and met his gaze squarely. Something in his gut told him the admission had cost her a great deal of pride.

"David," he corrected quickly. "Surely marrying gives us the right to forego the formalities of pomp and titles."

She colored and nodded, but a waitress arrived before she could respond, bearing a tray with two glasses of lemonade. It was not the same young woman who'd spilled the cake. This one nodded politely at them and disappeared as silently as she'd arrived.

"Very well, David." Elizabeth said his name shyly once they were alone again. Her tone indicated she was unsure of the sound and feel of his name in her mouth. No doubt, a woman of her upbringing felt like she was breaking a thousand proprieties to skip ahead to such intimacies. "I want to assure you there is no need to go to such extravagance on my behalf in the future." Her eyes flitted over his humble outfit and returned to his face. She gave him a tremulous smile. "I've learned how to make do on very little."

I reckon you have. Guilt stabbed his insides at the knowledge she'd jumped to the very conclusion he'd intended by dressing so shabbily for their first meeting as an affianced couple. Then again, he'd been hiding the true state of his finances ever since his arrival into Angel Creek. Everyone in town assumed he was poor, which couldn't be farther from the truth.

Though born and raised in the south, his family had wisely invested in railroads from coast to coast. He was a very wealthy man, a fact that had always made him a target for designing mothers of young marriageable daughters. Sometimes it was downright difficult to determine if a woman genuinely liked him for who he was instead of the size of his bank accounts. Strangely enough, it was exactly why he'd allowed the men in town to talk him into the outlandish notion of securing a mail-order bride for himself. If he married a woman he'd never met, there was no way she could be marrying him for his money. Or so he hoped...

"Fear not, Elizabeth." He was more than a little impressed by her honesty. "Sharing a small wedding feast will not put us in the poorhouse. We can economize to your heart's content in the coming days. After," he waggled a finger at her, "we purchase you some yardage for a new dress. Pardon me for pointing it out, but I'd rather not have my wife wearing one that looks as if two or three of her could climb inside it."

To his surprise, his attempt at brevity festered an anxious frown between her brows. "Or I can simply have it altered. That would cost far less."

"You do not sew." He observed that fact aloud without thinking and instantly wished he'd kept his thoughts to himself. *Once upon a time, you likely had an army of servants to do all those things for you, my lovely little belle.*

"I am learning," she returned a mite stiffly. "I am extraordinarily skilled at needlework. How much more difficult can it be to sew a whole dress?" She sounded so uncertain that he hid a grin.

As different as picking a basket of cotton as opposed to harvesting the entire field, from his point of view.

"I reckon it's not too difficult," he conceded, though he had no intention of watching her slave away for days on a project that size, not when he could well afford to buy her dozens of dresses. "Do you cook?" he inquired out of fascinated curiosity. He'd rather hoped to marry a woman moderately skilled in the domestic arts. It was just now dawning on him that this would not be the case with Elizabeth.

"I, ah...some." She glanced away from him, fixing her gaze on a distant object outside the picture window to his left. "We had to let our chef go, but he was able to give me a few lessons before he secured another position."

Your chef, eh? No, his pretty bride-to-be did not cook, either. She could probably plan a menu for an entire town, but she would be lost in the kitchen when it came to picking up an actual knife.

"Tell me about your family." He pounced on what he hoped was a safer topic.

She raised and lowered her shoulders. "It's just Mama and the girls now. Three younger sisters, to be precise. Their names are Grace, Lilly, and Magnolia. Mags for short." Her voice grew hushed, and she gave a vicious twist to her linen napkin. "Papa and my brothers didn't make it through the war."

Neither did her fiancé. He grimaced, wishing he'd chosen a more cheerful topic. "I am sorry—"

"You might as well know the truth," she interrupted, cheeks turning a cherry apple red. "I agreed to follow my friends to Angel Creek, because Mama could no longer afford another mouth to feed. Pray assure me you already suspected something of the sort. That you weren't expecting a woman with a dowry or a glittering family legacy."

"I did. I do." He held up his hands in surrender. "Pray forgive the many gauche directions our tête-à-tête has ventured off to. Apparently, the war has taken away my abilities to carry on a lighthearted conversation. Perhaps, as a southern belle, that is something you can tutor back into me?"

"Former southern belle," she murmured, but there was a hint of a smile tugging at her mouth. "The weather is always a safe topic."

"Except when it is miserably cold outside like it is this evening," he noted wryly.

"Except then." She chuckled. "Plus, you may chatter to no end about the latest opera, whoever is hosting the next ball or dinner party, and the forecast for next year's crop season."

He could tell she was in her element now. Her blue eyes twinkled with so much merriment one could almost forget how desperately plain her dress was.

Over her head, he watched the curtains part. Elijah's chef appeared in the opening, bearing a newly decorated cake. "What about a man who wishes to court a woman?" he inquired, sparing her a wink that he hoped would distract her a few seconds longer from the coming surprise. "What topics would you suggest for him, madame?"

"Poetry," she said softly. "Definitely poetry."

"'A thing of beauty is a joy forever,'" he quoted.

"Keats!" She spilled a beauteous smile over him and clapped her hands in excitement. "A man who knows Keats? Be still my heart!" She placed a hand dramatically over that organ.

"'A thing of beauty is a joy forever,'" he repeated. "'Its

loveliness increases; it will never. Pass into nothingness; but still will keep. A bower quiet for us, and a sleep.'"

At a nod from him, the chef delivered the wedding cake to their table with a gallant flourish. He bowed low to them. "May I be the first to congratulate the happy couple?"

"You may." David reached out to shake his hand. "The cake looks marvelous. I cannot thank you enough."

"You already have." The chef bestowed another princely bow on them. Next, he ushered a young male server forward who deposited a knife and a pair of white plates on the table. They nodded at each other and took their leave together like a pair of twin soldiers marching in unison.

Elizabeth's eyes glinted with moisture as she clasped her hands tightly beneath her chin. "Poetry and a magnificent cake. One might begin to think you are trying to impress someone, captain."

"I am," he confessed, watching her closely. "Am I succeeding?"

She nodded, making the tiny blonde spirals bounce against her temples and cheeks. "I am utterly amazed. I hardly know what to say. Did you really do all this for me, David?"

"I did it for my wife."

Her lips parted on a sigh. "How romantic to go to such effort for a woman you never met! Or rather, one you did not realize you'd already met."

"My wife, nonetheless. I am blessed beyond belief she turned out to be you."

She caught her breath and shyly scanned his features as if trying to determine whether he spoke the truth.

He took advantage of her moment of uncertainty to cut the cake and lay a slice on a plate for her. He slid it across the table in her direction, hoping she was fond of white icing and peach preserves.

"Dessert before dinner, eh?," she mused dreamily, picking up her fork. The color was high in her cheeks, and one smile after another flitted across her expressive features.

"Knowing I'm about to marry such a beautiful, accomplished woman feels a lot like dessert before dinner," he agreed.

She blushed in earnest this time. "I thought we already established the fact I am well versed in neither sewing nor cooking."

He served himself a slice of their wedding cake and forked a bite. "Methinks you more than even out the scales in intelligence, wit, and beauty."

She caught her breath as he leaned across the table to raise his fork to her lips. Eyes fastened on his, she leaned forward and took a bite. Then she closed her eyes on a sigh.

"Good?" he asked after a moment.

She nodded and reopened her eyes. "It is divine. My compliments to the chef."

Their pot roast arrived on a lavish tray surrounded by steaming vegetables. It was way more than two people could eat.

Alas, Elizabeth didn't eat near as much as he hoped she would, considering how loose her dress was hanging on her too-thin frame.

"Might I be so forward as to inquire about the size of the home we will be living in?" She laid down her fork, looking anxious again. "Perhaps it would have been best if I'd written you in advance about the dire state of things with my family. We had to sell our home and most of our furnishings, but there were some items Mama was unable to part with. Quite a few items, in fact. Her lifelong collection of linens, the family portraits, crystal candlestick holders that were a wedding gift to her and Papa, and other heirlooms that have been passed down for generations…"

His heart sank as she described her lengthy list of belongings he was certain would not fit in his two-room hunting cabin.

"What I am trying to say is, she is sending it all to me, David. It was the only way she could ensure everything would be kept in the family. The trunks are en route as we speak and will arrive in the next few days."

He nodded, mind racing over his options. After being raised in the south, he understood they weren't discussing a few random belongings that could eventually be discarded. These were rare and momentous items his new wife would never be able to part with. "How many trunks do you have coming?"

She dropped her gaze. "Fifteen in all."

Good heavens! "I see." He rubbed a hand across his rugged jawline. *This calls for a new plan.*

"Will that be a problem?"

You might say that. "None at all." He forced a smile. *I will have to build you a new house, sooner rather than later. That is all.* His parents would be overjoyed when they found out. Or they would be, after they got over their shock of learning he'd up and gotten himself married again — to a mail-order bride, no less! They'd been urging him to build a more permanent abode on his property in Montana, to put down roots.

Ultimately, they were hoping he'd take over the management of their western rail holdings. Already, they were funneling work in his direction, setting up meetings with potential investors in neighboring towns, as well as towns as far away as California. His next meeting was right on the Gold Coast, itself, a few weeks from now.

"I am so glad you have room for my things." Her shoulders relaxed. "I was a wee bit worried."

"I do." It was clear she was finished eating, so David folded his napkin. "If you'll excuse me a few minutes, ma'am." He rose. "I have a quick errand to run before we head to the church." His new plan involved getting a reservation at one of the local boarding houses. If his memory served, there were two — one on either side of the stage depot with Elijah's Eatery sandwiched in between. Surely in a town this small, at least one of them would have a room to spare on such short notice. Not only would a reservation at the boarding house give Elizabeth and him a place nearby to retire after their wedding ceremony, it would also allow him to negotiate a storage space indoors for her trunks that was located within carrying distance of the stage arrival area. Things like crystal candlesticks would fare much better indoors than in the icy temperatures of one of his barn lofts.

"Take your time, captain." She shivered and wrapped her arms around her middle. "I've no objections to lingering inside a bit longer where it's nice and warm."

He reached for her hand and raised it to his lips, bowing gallantly over her. "I shall return with haste, my lovely bride."

Chapter 3: The Wedding Ceremony

The moment David left The Eatery, Elizabeth wished she'd inquired into the whereabouts of his wagon where he'd tossed her travel bag. It would have been nice to freshen up and change into something more suitable for getting married in. She glanced down at her drab brown getup and sighed. *I reckon such things don't matter any longer, now that I'm marrying myself a poor Army captain.*

In that moment, the curtain to the alcove swished open.

"Elizabeth!" a familiar female voice cried.

She jolted and swiveled around in her seat. "Caroline?"

"Mercy me! There you are, love. We've been searching high and low for you ever since we heard the stage had arrived." Caroline swept into the room with Melody right on her heels, or what little she could see of her other friend. Her arms were loaded down with packages. "You sure didn't make it easy for us to find you." She paused and stared at the wedding cake. "Oh, my!" She shoved aside one drooping plume on her hat to get a better look at it.

"It's lovely, isn't it?" Elizabeth gave the cake a wistful

smile, knowing it was probably the last time she would get to experience such sweet extravagance. "Probably more than my groom can afford, but he seemed bound and determined to make a good first impression."

"Ha!" Caroline snorted and tossed her head, making the feathers on her hat bounce like ballerinas. "About the state of that man's finances... From what Melody and I have been able to determine, Mr. Pemberton went well out of his way, in fact, to make a false impression on you. On all of us, for that matter!" She grimaced. "And we reckoned you had a right to be warned."

Elizabeth's head waved between the two women, trying to gauge if they were serious.

Melody nodded vehemently from behind her packages. "It's true, my friend. Every word of it."

Every word of what? "I'm afraid I do not understand," she confessed.

"Of course you do not understand! It is exactly as he intended, to leave you purposefully in the dark. That was why we just *had* to find you before the wedding."

"Please." Elizabeth leaped from her chair, chest filling with dread. "If there is something you have against Captain Pemberton, now is the time to tell all — *before* I marry him."

Caroline glanced furtively around them. "For one thing, he is a liar."

No! Elizabeth felt as if she'd been stabbed. "How so?" Her impression of the captain was everything that was good. So much so that she didn't want to believe otherwise. Lord help her, she couldn't afford to believe otherwise. Why, that would leave her penniless and alone thousands of miles from home!

"He's been living in his family's tiny hunting cabin up creek a ways and driving around town in that rattletrap wagon of his. Clearly, he wanted the citizens of Angel Creek to think he was poor."

"But he's not poor?" *How in tarnation did you come to that conclusion?* A sliver of hope curled its way through Elizabeth's chest. Maybe there was still a God in Heaven, after all. If her soon-to-be husband wasn't as poor as she'd presumed...

"Far from it!" Melody cut in excitedly. "Caroline sent a telegram back home to verify her suspicions, and it arrived back with an answer just this morning."

"Saying..." Elizabeth prodded when the two women lapsed into silence.

Caroline slapped at the air. "While the south was losing the war, the Pembertons were steadily increasing their holdings in the northern rail lines, that's what!"

"And the western ones, to be fair," Melody added.

"It's the northern ones I'm most concerned about," Caroline snapped.

Elizabeth shook her head, utterly perplexed. "You say that like he's guilty of a crime."

"No? At the very least, he's guilty of not lifting a finger to help those we loved while they were perishing." Caroline's voice was bitter. "Think about it, Liz. Your father, brothers, and fiancé were busy giving their all, while that blasted man was profiting off Yankee commerce."

"His family might have invested in such a manner, regardless of the war." Elizabeth felt like she was grasping at straws, but she was loath to bury a man's character without giving him the slightest chance to defend himself.

"Perhaps, but his family should have invested in the southern railways, *because* of the war. If enough folks like him had made a different choice, why the war, itself, might have ended differently."

Would we have wanted that, when slavery is so morally repug-

nant? But Elizabeth knew the sentiments of her kind-to-a-fault friend had nothing to do with slavery. It was about their homes, their families, and everything they'd lost.

"Oh, Caroline," she cried softly. "We've all suffered. Immensely, my friend, but it's hardly fair to put the blame of the entire war at one man's feet. He wore a southern uniform and served our troops faithfully." She'd witnessed his service firsthand, as well as his suffering. He'd lost loved ones, too. Maybe not in battle, but it was no small thing to lose one's wife and unborn child.

Caroline rolled her eyes at Melody. "I told you she would defend the dashing captain, did I not? I knew it." She shook her head at Elizabeth. "I love you, darling, but you always did take up for the underdog. Are you entirely certain you want to go so far as to marry the lowdown scamp? It's not too late to change your mind. There are plenty of other men who'd be happy to marry someone as beautiful and talented as you. Right away, love, if you wish. Just say the word, and we'll whisk you down the street to your next beau in two snaps."

My next beau. Elizabeth's breath came out in an amazed huff. She truly had no interest in being handed off like a child's toy from one man to the other. "I really fail to see the downside of marrying a wealthy man." Her mind raced over the possibilities. Why, she might be able to send money home soon to Mama and the girls, if she went through with their nuptials.

Caroline pursed her lips. "True. When you put it that way, you might have a point. I suppose it would serve him right if you went along with the marriage for a few days — just long enough to get your hands on some of those ill-gotten Yankee profits of his."

"Caroline!" Elizabeth gasped. "That's not what I meant. How can you say such a thing?" This wasn't her friend talking. She wasn't seeing reason at the moment. It was the bitterness of all her pain and loss talking. Of all their mutual pain and loss…

"I'll say it, because your mama and sisters desperately need the money. They're one step away from losing everything."

"That is true, but—"

"So marry him if you insist. But only long enough to take back some of what is rightfully yours."

"Caroline, it's not like—"

"Do it, Elizabeth," Melody urged. "Do it for us all. For everyone of the menfolk we had to bury."

"Fine!" She sighed in resignation. "I'll marry him." She'd already planned to marry him, anyway. If her two friends chose to presume she was doing it for some deep-seated southern cause, then so be it. The end result would be the same. She would be a married woman by nightfall, no longer desperate for two pennies to rub together.

On the other side of the curtain, David's insides froze as he heard the horrific conversation of the women play out. For a moment there, it sounded like Elizabeth might actually be trying to defend him. He'd hoped against hope she would say something on his behalf to set her friends straight about his many years of loyal service to the Confederate Army. But her final callous agreement to marry him, despite his alleged sins against the south, was nearly his undoing. By all that was holy, this was the one thing he'd feared the most — being married for nothing more than his money.

So much for seeking out a beautiful southern belle who would erase his loneliness and become his lifelong friend and companion. He mentally scrambled to piece together his faint memories concerning the details of his mail-order bride agreement. The local men had tried to explain it. He had twenty or thirty days to consummate the marriage and make a go of things with Elizabeth. If theirs proved not to be a match made in heaven, however, either could annul the marriage before the end of the allotted trial.

Which he fully intended to do if he could not earn his bride's earnest admiration and respect for who he was. The real David Pemberton, a man in search of a restored purpose after the war and a staggering row of personal losses. A man who foolishly still believed in things like God, higher callings, and true love.

The curtain brushed aside, and the three women breezed past him in a swirl of puffy skirts and rose water, oblivious to his presence. For a few minutes, he feared Elizabeth's friends had indeed talked her out of marrying him. That he'd missed some vital piece of their conversation while reeling in shock and dismay outside the alcove…

They disappeared into the foyer and remained gone a good ten minutes or so. Hardly knowing what to do, he returned to their pre-wedding feast, leaned his elbows on the tabletop, and dropped his face in his hands.

Elijah's voice made him jump. "How was your dinner and your cake, captain?"

"Superb." He raised his head and spoke through stiff lips. "Will you package up the rest and send it next door to the Rose Haven? I'll be spending the night there." There was no point in canceling his reservation at the boarding house at this late juncture, even if he had to stay there alone.

"Right away, captain!" Elijah busied himself, collecting their plates and the platter. He returned a few minutes later to package up the wedding cake.

David pulled out a gold pocket watch that had belonged to his grandfather — may he rest in peace — and glanced at the time. His wedding was scheduled to take place a mere fifteen minutes from now, and his bride and her friends were nowhere in sight. He sighed and returned his watch to his pocket. There would be no union even to annul if there was no wedding ceremony this evening.

I shouldn't have listened to the likes of Adam Larsen. Spinning this whole mail-order proposition into something holiday festive and magical. Adam was one of the local ranchers, and not just any rancher. He was the new husband of Elizabeth's vocal friend, Caroline — another one of this year's mail-order brides from Charleston — the one who, most unfortunately, was busy trying to talk his own bride-to-be out of marrying him.

I reckon I'll just tuck my tail between my legs like a mangy dog and mosey my way back to my lonely existence. He couldn't wait for the night, and all its humiliation, to be over. Maybe he'd just hunt and live off his few hundred acres of land for the next few months, so he wouldn't have to flaunt his failure in front of the other new, happily married men in town any time soon.

The curtain rustled again. Wondering what Elijah could possibly be returning for now that the table was cleared, David glanced up and sat riveted.

Elizabeth had returned. Except she was no longer wearing the tattered brown dress she'd arrived in. She'd traded it in for a much newer, much more elaborate gown in many hues of rose and gold. She looked every inch of the high society debutante she'd once been. Her blue eyes glimmered across the alcove at him with a half-hopeful, half-wary light that he could thank Caroline and Melody for putting there. Rather notably, the gown fit her like a glove which could only mean one thing. She'd dressed as shabbily as he had on purpose for their first encounter. But to what end? She'd already confessed she was poor, that her family had lost nearly everything during the war. What else could she possibly have to hide from him?

It took a moment for him to recover his power of speech in the face of such loveliness. He leaped to his feet and strode around the table to hold out his hand to her. To his enormous pleasure, she placed her fingers in his. They were much warmer than before, and they trembled slightly, a fact that brought out every protective male instinct in him. It was surprising to witness her display of bridal nerves, considering the likelihood her reasons for marrying him were dubious, at best. He fought to swallow his disappointment at what might have blossomed between them without her friends' untimely interference.

"Your dress is lovely. Have your trunks arrived early, then?" He brought her hand to his mouth and brushed his lips across her knuckles.

She flushed and gave a small shiver that he didn't understand, given the toasty temperature of the room. "Not that I am aware. I borrowed this from my friend, Caroline Bishop. We're about the same size." She gave a nervous chuckle. "Well, technically, she is Caroline Larsen now. I'm still getting used to her married name."

"I am acquainted with her husband," he noted. "I'll be sure to thank them both. Adam for recommending I send off for a mail-order bride and Caroline for transforming my bride into a fairy princess."

"You can thank me now, captain." Caroline's cool but cultured voice wafted from behind the curtain. She reappeared and waved impatiently at them. "Come. Reverend Tilly is waiting for you. Best not to keep him waiting if you hope to say your vows this evening."

She didn't sound overly put out about the fact Eliza-beth had decided to stay the course and marry him. On the contrary, she looked gleeful, like a woman with a big, wonderful secret. It was way too bad her secret involved coaxing his soon-to-be-bride into siphoning off his fortune, then annulling their forthcoming marriage.

E lizabeth felt like she was walking in a dream, gliding slowly across the frozen, hard-packed earthen street on David's arm. As he had on their trek to The Eatery, he removed his coat and tucked it snugly around her shoulders. It was wonderfully warm from the heat of his shoulders, and it smelled like smoke and pine needles. For a moment, she imagined she was marrying a humble farmer in Montana instead of a wealthy rail investor.

Just as her teeth were starting to chatter from the biting cold, he ushered her up the stairs and inside the church building. Like Elijah's restaurant, the heat from a wood stove chased away the chill.

Once the doors were shut behind them, David drew her a few steps away from the others. "I must confess when you disappeared from our dining table, I feared you'd changed your mind about marrying me."

She shook her head slightly, making the white-blonde curls at her temples dance again. "As it stands, captain, you're fortunate enough to have chosen a bride who cannot afford her passage home." There was a teasing note to her voice that did not match the anxiety in her gaze.

"Hogwash!" He scowled in concern at her. "I will see to it you make it home to your family, if that is what you truly wish."

She gave him a tremulous smile. "I've come an awfully long way to back out now."

"Even so," he assured gently, taking her hands in his. "Now that we've met and conversed over dinner, if you're having any second thoughts whatsoever about getting married, now is the time to voice them. For both our sakes," he added beneath his breath.

She was struck at the uncertain ring to his voice. It mirrored her own feelings perfectly. Was he experiencing the same raw set of nerves twanging throughout her body? Was he equally overwhelmed at the earth shattering, life-changing step they were about to take together?

A lone pianist played the opening notes to the wedding march composed by Mendelssohn.

"It is time, David." Her words were barely above a whisper. "So unless you're the one having second thoughts about taking this spinster to be your lawfully wedded wife..."

"Spinster!" He arched his brows at her and treated her to such a comical look that she laughed. "You can't be a day over nineteen."

"I am two and twenty," she corrected with a grimace.

"Shocking!" He winked at her, not looking the least disturbed about her maturity. He tugged at her hands. "We'd best whisk you off the shelf, then, and hurry you down the aisle."

She shot him such a grateful look that it was all he could do not to kiss her right there in full view of their small crowd of witnesses.

Instead, he escorted her proudly down the aisle. For a small town on a cold evening, there were a decent number of folks gathered. Besides Caroline and Melody, their two husbands were present, along with the blacksmith, the saloon keeper, and several other men and women whose faces he did not recognize. He was still fairly new in town, only having arrived a little less than a year ago, and he'd spent precious little of that year socializing.

He and Elizabeth came to a halt in front of Revered Tilly. The pianist allowed the notes of the wedding march to fade.

"Dearly beloved," the reverend droned. "We are gathered here today to unite this man and this woman in holy matrimony." He dispatched a brief sermon on love and commitments, then had them recite their vows.

"I do." Elizabeth's face tilted up to his, looking and sounding sincere.

He allowed himself the luxury of imagining she was marrying him because she wanted to, despite her knowledge of his wealth and where it had come from.

"Now you may kiss the bride," Reverend Tilly announced brightly.

Maybe he was a fool for doing something so brash, but David threw all caution to the wind and wrapped his arms around Elizabeth's waist. He drew her against his chest and pressed his mouth to hers.

Her lips trembled beneath his, but he could have sworn she kissed him back.

"My wife," he muttered against the edge of her mouth. "Mine." He had no idea where his burst of possessiveness came from, only that he never wanted to stop kissing her.

"And you are mine," she returned softly, making his heart leap with exultation.

Hers. He suddenly and completely wanted to be exactly that — hers. He reluctantly raised his head and turned with her to face the townsfolk. A few of them were beaming their congratulations. A few of them were not. Caroline was among the few of them who were not.

He met her inscrutable stare and nodded. She was the first to look away.

The reverend produced a marriage certificate and bade them sign it. He wore a sleepy expression, as if he was in a hurry to complete the ceremony so he could get home and tumble into bed.

The moment David handed back the pen, he turned to his new bride. "Are you ready to head over to the boarding house, beautiful?"

She looked confused. "Aren't you going to take me home?"

He escorted her up the aisle, thinking about the rustic, unadorned cabin awaiting them in the woods. "How about I drive you to my property for a visit tomorrow? That way you can help me pick out the perfect place to build our new home."

It was a good thing they'd reached the doors of the church, because she blinked her beautiful blue eyes rapidly a few times. Then she burst into tears.

Chapter 4: Courting

DAVID

A ghast at Elizabeth's show of emotion, David hurried her outside to the street, shrugging out of his jacket for a third time that evening to tuck it around her shoulders.

"Please assure me you are well, darling," he pleaded, curling an arm around her shoulders. *Darling?* Where had that endearment come from? It had simply rolled off his tongue.

"I am, thank you." She nodded and blinked a few more times. This caused the first fat droplets to course their way down her cheeks. "It's just that I thought you were as poor as I am when we met earlier, but Caroline insists you are not. And now you're offering to build us a new home. My head feels like it's spinning off my shoulders right now."

There was no use denying her claim, now that his secret seemed to have jumped out of the bag on its own. "Caroline is right. You married a wealthy man. That is not normally a catalyst for such distress." His tone was frostier than he intended it to be.

"Agreed." She gulped and seemed to be trying to collect herself. "Normally, being blessed with wealth would be a cause for great rejoicing. What I do not understand is why you went to such lengths to hide it from me. A lack of honesty seems like a very poor foundation upon which to build a marriage." More tears gushed down her cheeks.

Good gravy! That was her take-away from his confession that he was a wealthy man? Tears and an accusation of dishonesty...*egad!* They'd been married all of a few minutes, and already he'd made her weep. Her show of distress made little sense, however, considering her own attempt at subterfuge.

"Perhaps my reasons were not so different from your own?" he offered testily. "I am beginning to think the shabby gown you arrived in isn't your own, after all."

"Technically, it does belong to me," she chided with an accusing, albeit tearful, glance up at his face. "Or, rather, it belonged to a former maid named Lucy. I found it in her bedchamber after I was forced to let her go due to our rapid change in fortune."

"And you wore it to meet me, because..." he prodded.

"For my own safety, of course!" she snapped. "I was forced to travel alone without a proper chaperone. It seemed best to dress in such a way as to draw as little attention to myself as possible."

"I see." Actually, he was stunned at her demonstration of such practical good sense. He guiltily thought of his own reasons for subterfuge, and they came up severely lacking compared to hers.

"I've told you my reasons. Now, what is your excuse for dressing so humbly?" She shot him an indignant glare through the moisture in her eyes. "For our wedding, no less! At least, I had the sense to bring along a change of clothing."

"The same reason I convinced myself to send off for a mail-order bride," he confessed ruefully. "The first time I was married, it was at the behest of my parents to form an alliance between two powerful rail investor families. This time, I wished to be married for...me," he finished lamely after a pause. "Is that such a horrible thing?"

Though her tears stopped flowing, she still looked puzzled. "I fail to see how you could hope to be married for the man you are on the inside while going to such lengths to hide your true self."

"Your logic is impeccable, I'm sure," he muttered, digging in the pocket of his trousers. He produced a clean white handkerchief. "Here. For the tears," he said gruffly, offering it to her.

She took it with a shiver and dabbed at her eyes and cheeks.

They ascended the stairs to the wide, front veranda of the Rose Haven, which was across the street and a little to the left of the church. Lining the porch wall were gray stone urns that bore the naked stems of rose bushes. They would be bursting with blooms again, come spring.

The boarding house was a simple two-story structure made of timbers weathered to a dull gray. However, ivy and rose vines climbed its walls, lending it an air of regal, old-world charm.

David opened the front door for her, and they stepped inside. The old-world charm continued into the parlor to their right. Pale blue velvet sofas were cozily arranged before a stone hearth that was leaping with flames. Just inside the entrance of the room was a cherry-wood pianoforte. Overlooking it was the painting of a frosty-haired man in his twilight years.

"That's my husband, may the good Lord rest his soul."

They spun around to face a spritely older woman, as

thin as a washboard with a pair of golden-hazel eyes that twinkled like the sun. Her hair rose in a white, fluffy pile atop her head. If it was any less curly, it might have passed for a bun. Instead, it waved this way and that as if to tell the world it couldn't be tamed.

"His name was Matthew, and he was one of the original founders of Angel Creek. I'm his widow, Martha Gable, and the owner of this fine establishment." She sounded proud, gracious, and welcoming — everything a boarding house proprietress should be.

"Pleased to meet you, ma'am." Elizabeth held out a dainty hand.

"The pleasure is all mine, to be hosting a pair of newlyweds." Widow Gable ignored her hand and swept her into a hug. "Why, I couldn't have been more delighted when your husband approached me about it earlier. Be assured I've put the two of you in my best room." She held Elizabeth at an arm's length away. "I call it the Honeymoon Suite. Has its own sitting area, balcony, and tub."

Elizabeth's startled gaze flew to David's as the tiny woman marched them across the foyer and up a flight of wooden stairs. "You mean for us to stay the night here? Together?" she hissed to him as they walked.

He nodded, thoroughly bemused at the sudden return of her bridal nerves.

"Wouldn't we have more, er...space if you simply took me home?"

"No," he returned bluntly. "The truth is, I've been living in a minuscule hunting cabin on the land I inherited from my grandfather. Trust me. This suite is much larger and much better furnished."

Widow Gable must have overheard his last statement, because she flung a smile over her shoulder. "There's no finer place to stay in town, if I do say so myself, and nothing half as romantic for newlyweds." She led them down a hall with three doors on one side and three doors on the other. She opened the door in the middle, leading to a room in the front portion of the second story. "Welcome home, my dears."

She ushered Elizabeth and David inside, while remaining in the doorway. "The tub is behind the Chinese screen." She pointed to the brightly embroidered tapestry in the far corner of the room that separated the bathing area from the sleeping area. "Just ring that chain against the wall for room service when you want your bath drawn. As for sustenance, we serve breakfast, lunch, and dinner in the dining room downstairs. Or, again, you are welcome to call room service and have it delivered here." She waved her gnarled hand at a tiny table for two in one corner of the room. "Don't forget Elijah sent over what was left of your wedding cake and dinner from The Eatery. Oh, and your bags are unpacked. Everything is hanging inside the wardrobe or setting inside the drawers next to the basin."

Elizabeth looked amazed. "I thank you." No one had unpacked for her since her mother had sold their family home and let all their servants go.

"My pleasure." Widow Gable industriously smoothed her gingham skirts. "Do you have any questions of me before I give you your privacy?" She smiled knowingly at David and shot him a saucy wink behind Elizabeth's back.

He smiled at her but said nothing.

"No, ma'am. This is quite perfect," Elizabeth said in a faint voice. She'd gone to stand in front of the large picture window facing the street. "Why, there's a door behind the curtain!" she exclaimed.

"It leads to the balcony," Widow Gable announced in pride. "You'll find it provides a pretty view of the town; and what's more, you'll have it all to yourselves."

Soon they were left standing alone in the widow's prized honeymoon suite.

"Would you care for me to ring us up a pot of tea or any other refreshments?" he inquired politely of his new bride. It was clear her case of bridal nerves was growing more acute. He'd been expecting this. It had been much the same with his first wife.

Elizabeth whirled in his direction so swiftly, it made her full skirts swirl around her shoes, revealing a pair of silk stockings and elegantly curved ankles. She flushed beneath his perusal and flounced her skirts to settle them back in place. "Pray do not try to pretend this isn't awkward for both of us."

He raised his brows at her.

"For me," she amended with a pretty little scowl he found endearing, though he was sure it was meant as anything but.

"Pray explain yourself." He tried not to think of how tired he was and how lush and comfortable the mattress looked, since it wasn't likely he'd be enjoying it.

"Beautiful furnishings, m-mind you," she spluttered, "but an utterly awkward situation, nonetheless." She waved a hand in exasperation at the four-poster bed. It was covered in a cheerful quilt of winter whites and pale, snowy blues. The canopy was drenched in more of Widow Gable's signature white lace that seemed to be in every room of the boarding house. "For one thing, there is only one bed."

"Most married couples sleep together," he pointed out, "but if you wish otherwise, I can sleep on the floor."

Her aghast gaze dropped to the hardwood planks. "It looks mighty uncomfortable down there."

"Do you have any better ideas?" he inquired mildly. He crossed the room to remove his jacket from her shoulders.

"I reckon we'll both be sleeping in the bed," she conceded, sending a half-fearful, half-mortified look in its direction.

He was so surprised at her offer that he didn't answer right away.

"Well, what is it to be?" she snapped.

"It's a big bed," he noted. "If I stay on my side, you'll never know I'm there." It was a lie, of course. They would be very much aware of each other's presence.

She made a sound of frustration. "I could really use a bath, but I've never had an audience for that before. I, er, I don't believe I'm ready for one, either."

He gave her what he hoped was an understanding smile. "How about I ring for room service, then make myself scarce while you bathe?"

She nodded, looking relieved. "I thank you."

He surprised them both by leaning forward to kiss her on the cheek. "I'll return in an hour. You have my full approval to miss me horribly." He meant it, too. She was turning out to be such a delight to tease that he was loath to leave her.

She rolled her eyes and gave him a gentle shove. "You'd best mosey on out the door, so I can start missing you, then."

When he returned to their chamber, she was tucked snugly beneath the thick winter quilt, dressed in a pale pink nightgown, silk if he wasn't mistaken, and she was fast asleep. Her blonde hair was unbound and tumbling in waves around her shoulders and across her pillow. Heavenly days! She was as beautiful asleep as she was awake. Maybe more so.

A quick trip behind the Chinese screen proved her bath water had not been drained, and it was still warm. *Thank God for small miracles!* Since his wife was so soundly asleep, he stripped down and stepped into the tub. Reaching for the soap, he slicked away the miles of the road he'd accumulated over the last few days. Ah, but it was good to be clean again! When he was finished bathing, he dried himself and donned a clean change of clothing. No need to frighten his new bride by coming to bed in a robe.

He stirred the fire in the hearth and added another log to keep the room as warm as possible. Then he climbed into bed beside her, trying to make as few movements as possible so as not to disturb her.

To his surprise, she murmured something in her sleep and rolled away from him the moment his long limbs settled on his side of the bed. Her movements brought her dangerously close to the edge of the mattress.

"Elizabeth," he called softly. He rolled to his side to tap her shoulder. "Wake up, darling." Again, the endearment came from nowhere, catching him off guard. *My darling, eh?* Married for one evening to a woman he wasn't sure he even wanted to stay married to, and already he was growing affectionate.

He tapped her gently on the shoulder again, hating to rouse her from her sleep, but he hated the thought of her tumbling over the side of the bed, even more.

She brushed away his hand. "I have to go, Mama," she said sharply. "It's up to me now to find—" Her words ended in a muffled shriek as she started to roll over the side of the bed.

David lunged in her direction and looped his arm around her waist in the nick of time. Not knowing what else to do, he tugged her back against his chest and spooned his body around hers. "It's alright, love. I have you," he crooned.

She wriggled feverishly within his embrace. "What is going on?" she gasped.

He immediately removed his arm from around her and rolled back to his side of the bed. "You almost fell to the floor."

"Good gracious!" She sat up, rubbing her arms in agitation. "It must have been another one of my nightmares."

"Do you have them often?" Sympathy tugged at his chest. Many of his soldiers had been plagued by nightmares after all they'd seen and endured – so much so that some of them feared going to sleep. As a battlefield nurse, she'd experienced many of the same horrors.

"Now and then," she muttered. She shot him an anxious look. "Did I say anything?" By the light of the flickering fire, he could discern she was blushing in mortification. "My sisters say I talk something awful when I'm having nightmares." She chuckled. "They claimed they could carry on a whole conversation with me, sometimes."

"Nothing at all," he lied, recalling her words. *I have to go, Mama. It's up to me now to find…* Was she reliving her decision to go search for her fiancé who was missing in battle? If so, did that mean she was still in love with him?

He tried to recall the man's name…Charles something. Perhaps David was being callus by not discussing her nightmare with her in more detail, but he saw no point in reliving the past. Every man she had ever loved or contemplated marrying was either a ghost or a distant memory. He was her husband now.

"May I get you anything? I could ring for a pot of hot tea." He'd offered it earlier in the evening, but she'd ignored him.

"Yes," she whispered. "I think I'd like that cup of tea, now."

He rolled out of bed to pull the chain against the wall. "Anything for my lovely new bride," he teased, hoping to lighten the mood in the room. "Come." He beckoned to her. "Sit with me for a spell." He figured she wasn't ready to go back to sleep just yet. Not with the shadows of her darker memories still lurking.

She gave a sigh of resignation, then slipped from the bed. Joining him on the short sofa by the fire, she tugged the edges of her robe more tightly around her, looking self-conscious. "I don't suppose this is the way you imagined spending your wedding night."

"I've no complaints." Sensing she needed reassuring, he scooted closer to her on the sofa and slid an arm around her.

To his surprise and delight, she tipped her head against his shoulder. "Thank you for understanding." She sounded so apologetic that he couldn't help wondering if she was referring to the fact she wasn't ready to be his wife in every sense of the word.

As much as he would have enjoyed it, he didn't mind waiting. He'd just as soon be more sure about her reasons for marrying him in the first place before consummating their union.

For now, he was content to breathe in her soapy scent while cuddling her against his side. He closed his eyes, trying to imagine what it would be like if she was truly in love with him. What it would feel like to be held by her, kissed by her. Lord help him, but that was a dangerous direction for a man's thoughts to run! It was all he could do not to turn his face and bury his nose in her hair.

A knock sounded. Grateful for the diversion, he disengaged himself from her warm, slender frame to open the door. It was their tea.

He thanked Widow Gable and promised not to trouble her any more that evening. Then he strode across the room to set the tray on the small trestle table next to the sofa. As he poured two steaming cups, the scents of cinnamon and pumpkins filled the room.

"Tea is served, darling." He held one of the white porcelain teacups out to her.

She cupped it in both hands and held it to her nose, breathing deeply. "Does all your marvelous attentiveness mean you're courting me, David Pemberton?"

He made a snorting sound. "Nothing gets past you, does it, beautiful?"

Chapter 5: Shocking News

ELIZABETH

E lizabeth enjoyed the next few weeks she and David got to spend at Rose Haven, more than she imagined possible. Her enormous pile of trunks arrived. Overjoyed to be reunited with her beloved treasures, she tried not to think what it had cost her mother in shipping fees. Or how her mother had managed to scrounge up the funds, for that matter...

Widow Gable allowed them to stack Elizabeth's trunks in one of the empty suites across the hall. She refused to charge them any extra for it, claiming it was space not being used, anyway. She doted on them with the same indulgent pride as if they were her son and daughter. Apparently, she and Matthew had never been blessed with any children of their own.

"I'll be sorry to see you go, dearies. I've never enjoyed a set of guests more," she sighed. "Mind you, I'm as happy as a pony in a field of oats about the new home you're building. Perhaps, you'll find it in your heart to invite me over for tea when it's finished?"

"Most certainly." Elizabeth was all shades of giddy

with joy over the construction of their house. She'd already written Mama and her sisters, begging them to visit the moment it was ready to move into. She had to keep pinching herself to make certain she wasn't dreaming, having gone from a penniless pauper to a pampered princess the evening she'd stepped foot in Angel Creek.

To top it all off, her prince was kind and attentive, courting her like the most debonair of beaux. He managed to acquire a new gilded carriage and took her out for a ride every afternoon during the warmest part of the day. Usually, they drove out to his homestead to check on the progress of their construction project.

"Twenty-one days," Elizabeth sighed, gazing out their carriage window at the timbers forming their two-story home. It was only a little over a month until Christmas. The first snowfall was dusting the ground in front of the structure. In the distance, a whole forest of pines, spruces, and evergreens rose like watchful sentinels. If a person sat quietly enough, they could hear the distant rushing of the water in Angel Creek. According to the locals, it would soon freeze over, altogether.

"That's how long we've been married," David noted softly.

"You're counting, too?" She whirled to face him so quickly that the feathers in her hat brushed his nose.

He pretended to scowl at her. "Of course. It's how long I've been weighed down with the enormous responsibility of managing myself a southern bride."

"Managing?" she exclaimed in mock outrage. "Managing!" She balled up her gloved hands and launched herself at him, pummeling his shoulders and chest.

He caught her fists and used them to tug her closer. "Yes, managing. See what I have to put up with?" His head dipped lower over hers, bringing his lips a shallow breath away from her mouth.

It was the closest he'd come to kissing her since their wedding ceremony. Her heartbeat raced at the way his gaze was burning into hers. "You poor, poor creature," she crooned. "A quiet, brooding rail man shackled to a sassy girl from Charleston. No doubt the whole town sympathizes with your plight." Some of the merriment evaporated from her at the recollection that a few of her friends remained none too thrilled about her marrying a man who'd invested in northern railways during the war.

"Perhaps you could console me with a kiss," he urged huskily. "Surely, twenty-one days of courting has earned me one tiny kiss?"

She quickly stretched her neck to peck him on the tip of his nose. "There. One tiny kiss. Does that suffice?"

"Not even close." With that, he hauled her against his chest and sealed his mouth over hers. Her fancy new hat went tumbling somewhere on the carriage seat behind her as he splayed a hand between her shoulder blades to draw her closer still. "My lovely bride," he murmured between kisses. "My sweet, beautiful Elizabeth."

His words of endearment took her breath away. "David," she whispered. "Does this mean you've come to care for me at least a little?"

He abruptly raised his head from hers. "Do tell! Did I say something to give it away?" His voice was teasing, but his expression was deadly serious as he searched her face.

"But we've just met."

"We've more than met, darling. We're married, in case you've forgotten." He tucked a stray curl behind her ear.

"I haven't forgotten." She reached up to cup his cheek wonderingly. "It's just that these things take time. I can't tell you how much I appreciate the fact you haven't tried to rush into, well...you know." She blushed and ducked her head.

He pressed one long finger beneath her chin to tip her face back up to his. "We've conversed and dined and shopped together. We've slept in the same bed for three weeks. Every bloke in town who sees us together envies me my good fortune. I'd say that's long enough for any man to grow a little attached to his very beautiful, very intelligent, very talented bride."

She shook her head at him, though she couldn't hide a grateful smile. "What talents? I can't cook or sew to save my hide or yours."

He leaned forward to nuzzle his nose against hers. "I've heard you sing when you thought no one was listening. I've also witnessed your skill on the pianoforte in the parlor. Then there's the way you've managed to turn our small boarding house suite into a home — right down to that artful arrangement of pine bows and cones in the center of our table. Oh, and there's my heart." He brushed his lips over hers. "You make me happy, Elizabeth. If it's too soon to admit that, then so be it. It's true, and I'm not taking it back."

She yearned to believe him, yet... "Oh, David!" she sighed, as more reservations flooded her mind.

"Yes, darling?" He brushed his lips over hers again.

"Are you quite certain I'm not just filling a void in your life? Blotting out your loneliness? Making you not miss... her quite so much?" She shuddered to bring up the topic of his late wife. They'd not talked about the tragic woman before, nor her own dearly departed fiancé, Charley.

"You are doing every one of those things, for sure." He frowned slightly as he regarded her. "You fill an enormous void I didn't think would ever be filled again. Though my first marriage was an arranged one, I was lucky enough to be matched to a good woman. One I respected and became fond of over time. When she wrote me that she was expecting our first child, I was overjoyed — the kind of joy that got me through the darkest days of the fighting. When you sought me out at camp seven months later to tell me it was over, I thought my whole life was over."

"I'm so sorry that I had to be the one to bear such tragic news." Feeling like a nurse all over again, she cuddled him closer to soothe. She ran her hands up his chest and shoulders before twining her arms around his neck. *Maybe not like a nurse, after all. More like a wife.* She adored the fact that he was hers to hold and kiss and care for. She just needed some assurance, just a wee bit, that it was more than his loneliness speaking when they were together like this.

"I could see it in your face when you told me." His lips twisted at the memory. "It like to broke your heart, even though we'd never met before then."

Tears burned behind her eyelids. "Delivering news like that to our brave, young soldiers was, by far, the hardest part of my job. All the way to your tent, I prayed for a miracle. That one of the couriers would race up to me before I gave you the news and tell me it was all a horrible misunderstanding. An error in communication."

"Afterwards, I marveled about how much you seemed to care for my wellbeing in that moment, especially when I discovered you were in the midst of searching for your missing fiancé. To be suffering so much, yourself, and still care about the suffering of others..." He shook his head. "You are truly an amazing woman, Elizabeth Pemberton."

She jolted at the sound of her married name. "I'm still getting accustomed to my new name," she confessed.

He made a tsk-ing sound. "Do not try to sidetrack me,

Mrs. Pemberton. I believe we were discussing my growing regard for you."

She caught her breath. "So you think it's more than me filling a void in your life?"

He made a snorting sound. "I know it's more. Tarnation, woman!" He tightened his arms around her. "I might not have the perfect words to describe my feelings, according to the standards of a proper southern debutante, but that doesn't make what I feel for you any less real. I'm a grown man. I think I know my own heart."

"And I know mine." She rested her head on his shoulder.

"Elizabeth," he groaned. "You can't just lay something like that on a man, then hide your face, lass."

"But I'm comfortable here." She chuckled and burrowed her head against his neck. "If you must know, I have feelings for you, too."

"Oh, my darling!" He pressed his cheek to the top of her head. "Does this mean you're ready to take the next step? To make our union the permanent kind?" His voice was rough with emotion.

"Against the advice of all my well-meaning friends? Yes. I care for you, David, and I want to make this a real and lasting marriage." There. The truth was out at last. She'd been wanting to bare her soul to him for weeks. It was a relief to finally do so.

He grew still. "I reckon the advice of your friends concerns my railway investments during the Great War?"

"Your blasted Yankee sympathies, according to one of my friends."

"Are you accusing me of something, Elizabeth?"

She raised her head. "Surely, you jest. I observed you on the battlefield, remember? I know firsthand which side you fought for. What you risked every day. What it cost you to stay the course, while someone else lowered your loved ones back home into the ground. No, captain, I'm not accusing you of anything other than being a good man. A loyal soldier." She let out a weary expulsion of air. "I am sorry for my friends' misplaced distrust and hope we can win them over, in time. They've lost so much, David. It's human nature, methinks, to want to lay the blame on someone. You're simply a convenient target."

"Thank you, Elizabeth." He glanced away from her, mouth working with emotion. "I had to ask. I had to know after overhearing your conversation with your friends in the minutes leading up to our wedding."

"Oh, dear heavens!" She felt suddenly lightheaded, recalling exactly how deplorable their conversation had been. "Please, please, please assure me that — all this time — you haven't been thinking I married you for your wealth."

"I had my fears," he admitted with a rueful scowl. "Although it helped that you tried to defend me somewhat to them."

"Oh, David," she moaned faintly. "I am so sorry for putting you through such unnecessary worry. I didn't agree with what was being said, but I also understood where their sentiments were coming from. Like I said, they've suffered so much. We all have."

"Speaking of which, I've been meaning to ask you something else." His scowl deepened. "Something highly personal that I hope is my business to ask, now that we are married and plan to stay married."

She raised her brows at him, cringing on the inside. "Did I say something horrendous in my sleep?" She shuddered. "Please say no!"

"No." He chuckled and swooped in for another kiss.

"I'm trying to be serious, but you always seem to know how to make me laugh."

"Fine." She schooled her expression. "I'll be serious, too, but not for long; so you better talk fast."

His smile widened. "It's about your mother and sisters."

Her smile slipped. "Oh?"

"On the night we met, you were very honest about a few matters concerning the state of things with your family."

She bit her lower lip. "I shouldn't have burdened you with such things on the day of our wedding."

He shrugged. "We can quibble about the timing, or we can face the facts. Now that we are going to stay married, your burdens are my burdens, Elizabeth."

She stared at him in disbelief for the space of several heartbeats. "Y-you would help them? Truly, David?" She was so overcome with gratitude, she burst into tears.

"Truly, truly, Elizabeth." He gathered her in his arms and hugged her tightly.

All remaining doubts about their marriage disappeared. She clung to him like a lifeline. He was her rock, her strength, the man the good Lord had sent to save her family from starvation or worse. She was so grateful, she could have kissed his shiny, polished boots. Instead, she was going to become his wife — his real wife — this evening. She was going to love him and devote herself to him. She was going to defend him to her friends. She was doing to be the best rail investor's wife who'd ever set foot in Montana.

"Take me home, David."

He let go of her long enough to rap on the carriage wall. It was his signal to his driver, Sam Bullock, that they were ready to return to the Rose Haven. Then he gathered her close once more.

Though the wind was picking up outside their windows and the snow was falling thickly, Elizabeth knew they were in the best of hands with Sam driving David's team of horses. Sam had turned out to be much more than a driver. He'd served in David's household while David was growing up, then had followed him into battle. During the war, he'd cared for his master's laundry, mending, the upkeep of his tent and furnishings, as well as the treatment of an occasional wound. She'd never met a more loyal servant, and he'd wordlessly passed on that loyalty to her.

When David handed her down from the carriage at the front steps of the Rose Haven, she sent his driver a grateful smile. "Thank you, Sam. Now go inside and get warm for the night." He was staying in a loft room at the livery where David was boarding his horses. "I'll have Widow Gable send something down the street for your dinner." If she correctly recalled, there was venison stew on the menu this evening.

"Much obliged, Missus Pemberton." He tipped his hat at her and treated her to a lopsided grin.

David hustled her up the porch stairs with an arm curled around her shoulders.

"Someone might see us and suspect something," she muttered in embarrassment. "What with the way you're looking at me and all."

He chuckled and pressed a warm kiss to her chilly cheek. "Lawd 'a mercy, Elizabeth Pemberton! The things you worry about. To think the townsfolk might actually guess that I adore my wife. Oh, the horror!"

"You know what I mean," she admonished severely but spoiled the effect with a giggle.

They entered the boarding house in a swirl of icy wind and snowflakes.

"There you are!" Widow Gable snapped to her feet from her chair in the parlor beside the fire. "I've been waiting and waiting *and waiting* for you." She cast an anxious look at the window. "I couldn't believe how long you stayed out with the storm blowing in."

As much as Elizabeth appreciated everything their proprietress had done to make their stay a comfortable one, her heart sank at the sight of her. Usually when one became embroiled in a conversation with Martha Gable, it took a while. The woman could just about talk a body's arms and legs plumb off.

"We're here, safe and sound, as you can see." She raised a finger. "If I could please place an order for some of your stew to be delivered to the livery this evening. Sam was looking mighty hungry when he drove the horses away." There. That should give the widow something to attend to, something that wouldn't require her lingering overly long in the foyer.

"I'll be sure to do exactly that," Mrs. Gable assured, but her usual smile did not reappear and she did not immediately make her way down the hall towards the kitchen.

"Is there something else, ma'am?" David inquired politely, though Elizabeth could sense he was as impatient as she was to be alone with her upstairs.

"There is, captain." Widow Gable dug in her apron and unearthed a sealed envelope. "It's a letter for Elizabeth. Marked urgent." She held it out.

"From whom?" She snatched it up, heart leaping into her throat. There weren't very many folks in the world who would be writing her. "It's from home." She drew a deep breath and cast an anxious glance up at David. "Maybe I should read this in our room."

He nodded, looking concerned.

"I'll send up a pot of tea and some of my stew," the widow called after them.

Elizabeth didn't answer. Her heart was too busy pounding with dread with each stair she mounted. What could Mama have to tell her that was urgent? Elizabeth had seen to it they'd paid their next two months of rent before she departed home. There was no way Mama and her sisters were being evicted. Not yet, at least.

David opened the door to their suite and gently nudged her inside. "Sit," he commanded. "I'll get the fire going again."

She sat on the edge of the sofa and blindly watched him stir the dying embers. "I'm afraid to open it," she confessed in a voice barely above a whisper. "I can't take any more bad news, David. I just can't." In the past couple of years, her family had suffered as many setbacks as could be expected of a single family unit. Hadn't the good Lord, Himself, promised He wouldn't put on anyone more than they could bear?

"Would you like me to read it first?"

She shook her head. "No, it is something I must do."

"Would you care to read it aloud, darling, so we can bear it together?"

She nodded, gulping. "That I can do." With that, she tore open the envelope and hastily scanned the first few lines. "Merciful heavens!"

Her fingers were momentarily paralyzed and lost their grip, letting the paper flutter to her lap.

"Elizabeth?" David dropped the tong he was using to stir the embers. He rose from his knees to crouch in front of her. "Elizabeth! Speak to me. What is it, darling?"

She stared at him blindly for a moment. His handsome, worried features wavered in and out of focus a few times. "It's Charley!" she gasped.

"The man you were to marry?" He reached for her hands, frowning in alarm.

She nodded, eyes filling with terrified tears. "Mama says he's alive!"

Chapter 6: New Home

DAVID

David felt like his whole world was crumbling again — just like it had when Elizabeth delivered the tragic news of his wife and son's deaths. He rocked back on his heels, trying to absorb the mighty blow. After suffering such deeply personal losses, reuniting with Elizabeth had felt like fate. Marrying her had felt like a divine intervention, a healing of past wounds, a restoration of all he had lost. Elizabeth had entered Angel Creek, brightening his existence like the final victorious chapter of Job in the Bible.

And now this…

"May I read it?" He hardly recognized the harsh tone as his own voice.

She nodded, eyes wide with shock like she'd seen a ghost. If what her mother was claiming was true, she'd be laying eyes on one soon, as well.

The letter was brief and shattering.

My dearest Elizabeth,

I wrote the moment I found out and can only hope and pray my letter is not too late. I tried to send a telegram but was told no service runs as far as Angel Creek. Oh, my darling child! Charley is alive. He is alive and well. The remains of the man you buried were those of his brother, James. The mistake is understandable, considering how extreme his injuries were and the fact that Charley remained missing for so long. He suffered a head wound that left him oblivious as to who he was for the better part of two years. He's been in a hospital in Virginia all this time, struggling to remember his very name. What a miracle that our merciful God saw fit to restore him, body and soul, to us. You must come home, my precious girl. Charley has promised to take care of us after you are wed. There is no longer a need to throw your life away on a stranger you never met. Whatever you might have already done, please undo it. We anxiously await your return.

All my love,
Mama

David wanted to wad the letter up and throw it in the fire. He wanted to stomp around the room and throw things. Or punch something... *It's over between us, isn't it?* Not that he didn't rejoice in the fact that a soldier had returned alive and well from war, but the timing of this particular soldier's return couldn't have been worse.

He stared drearily at Elizabeth. *I won your heart and lost it in the same afternoon.* They'd never even gotten around to consummating their marriage, which meant she could have it annulled with no impediments.

It was a long time before either of them spoke again. Elizabeth went first in a voice that shook. "I don't know what to do. What to even say. It sounds as if Mama never received my last letter, telling her I was already married."

David glanced at the darkening light outside their window. They would need to light a lantern soon. "It's not safe to travel, but I'll find some way to get you home, if that is what you wish."

She blinked at him in the gathering shadows. "You would let me go?" Her question ended on a strange squeak. "Just like that?"

"If it is what you wish," he repeated coldly. No longer able to meet her gaze, he dropped her hands and returned to stoking the fire. "Tell me what you want, Elizabeth, and I will do everything in my power to make it happen."

"You're referring to our marriage, aren't you?" Her voice shook harder. "You think I'm going to leave you." She made a small choking sound that had him whirling in her direction. "Because of Mama's letter."

"Aren't you?" He dashed across the room to the decanter of water they always kept on a nightstand and poured her glass. He returned to her and pressed it in her hands. "You have every right to, you know, both morally and legally. You love him. You were promised to him."

"But I married you." The glass shook so badly in her grasp that she spilled some of the water on her lap. "I said my vows to you, David, and I meant them. Every word. I care for you now."

He withdrew the glass from her hands and held it to her lips. "Drink, please." As much joy as her words gave him, he needed her to calm down, to think with her head and not just her heart. To be very sure before she made such a monumental decision.

She choked down a sip, coughed, and tried again. "Enough." She pushed the glass away. "If you think I should go, I'll go, but I would prefer to have you by my side when I do. You're my husband, David. You and no other."

Hope burgeoned in his chest. He abruptly set the glass on the floor and took a seat beside her on the sofa. "Elizabeth, you could have our marriage annulled. I won't try to stop you."

Hurt clouded her gaze, turning it a tumultuous shade of blue. "Is that what *you* want, David?"

"No, I—"

"Then quit pushing me away," she snapped. "I know Mama's letter is shocking, and I have no idea what to do about her request at the moment." She flung a hand towards the window. "What I do know is, it's not safe to travel that far this time of year, so I'll not be having you or Sam risking life and limb to escort me anywhere for the time being. Nor will I for one second sit here and pretend like this will be the last or biggest challenge we will have to face as a married couple. We can't just run from our problems or give up every time our path gets a little rough."

With every word of her rant, David fell further and further beneath her spell. "Yes, ma'am," he said softly, when at last he could get a word in. "I'll not be pushing you away any longer, my feisty southern belle." She was his heart, his hope, his biggest reason for climbing out of bed each morning.

"Thank you!" She flung her arms around his neck and buried her face against his throat. "Because leaving you is the very last thing I want to do."

My darling wife! "I love you," he muttered into her hair.

She grew still in his arms. "Wh-what did you say?"

"I love you. So much that when I read your mother's letter, I felt like every word was ripping my heart out by the roots!"

"I love you, too, David." She raised her head and

sought out his lips. "Make me yours. Right now, please. That way we never, ever again have to talk about annulments or leaving each other or—"

With a cry of exultation, he swept her up in his arms and carried her to their bed, where he gently and tenderly did exactly what the mistress of his heart had commanded.

Many hours into the night, Elizabeth awakened to the howling of the winds outside the boarding house windows. She snuggled closer to her husband beneath the quilts.

He lazily reached over to tangle a hand in her hair. "Are you cold, darling?"

She pushed up on one elbow to squint across the room. A fire was leaping in the hearth, which meant he must have risen at some point to keep it going. "I've never been warmer." She chuckled softly and leaned over him to press her forehead to his. "Tell me again how much you love me." Her long tresses slid down to form a curtain around their faces.

He wrapped his arms around her and tumbled her atop him. "I married such a greedy, demanding wench," he muttered against her lips. "Is this what I have to look forward to?"

"Every day," she said happily, "for the rest of our lives."

He kissed her hungrily, like he was never going to stop. "Promise?"

"I promise, sweetheart."

The next morning, David helped her compose the most difficult letter she'd ever penned in her life.

Mama dearest,

I received your letter and am overjoyed to learn that Charley has returned to town. I am so thankful he is safe and well. His parents must be ecstatic to have one of their sons restored to them, please God.

And now for my own joyous news: I am a married woman, Mama. I married Captain David Pemberton the day I arrived to Angel Creek. Did you not receive my last letter, informing you of my nuptials? I am deeply sorry if it got misrouted. Please know that I am very happily married. David is working hard to get us a new house built on his property, and we hope you will visit us and stay a spell when it is finished — all of you. My sisters would have the most wonderful time here, getting to see so many friends again who have moved up this way. I miss you more than words can say. Since the roads are much too treacherous for travel this time of year, I shall go ahead and wish you a very Merry Christmas! I cannot wait to see you again.

All my love,
Elizabeth

Now that the secret was out about the true state of David's finances, he didn't bother hiding it any longer. Quite the opposite. He lavished so many gifts on his bride that she started to feel guilty.

"You've done enough," she protested one afternoon. He'd commissioned not one new dress, as originally promised on their wedding day, but three so far. Plus a riding habit, two hats, sturdy black boots, a pair of high-heeled dancing slippers, a crocheted reticule, and so many other odds and ends that she lost count of them. "You are positively spoiling me."

"Every man has a hobby." He winked at her. "Mine happens to be pleasing my wife."

"I am pleased. More than pleased. You can cease and desist your spendthrift ways at once, sweetheart, with my blessing." Why, the money he'd spend on one dress alone would have fed her mother and sisters for months!

He arched a brow at her. "I do not consider it a waste to dress my wife in style. Can't blame a man for enjoying the sight of someone so beautiful in a gown or two or three."

"Or three is right," she corrected tartly, "and that's if I don't count my new riding habit, coat, or cloak."

They were back in their boarding house room for the evening, having spent a very blustery afternoon at the homestead. The walls were going up slower than they'd hoped, since it was too cold and windy for the workmen to stay outside for much longer than an hour at a time.

David removed the black top hat he'd worn to their dinner at the hotel across town and sent it sailing across the room. It landed neatly on their bed. "It will be four if you count the nightgown of silk and lace I ordered this afternoon while you were selecting your next book from the mercantile." He shook his head at her growing collection of volumes on the mantle. "Our home isn't finished being built, and already I'm having to plan the addition of a library."

"Please don't," she begged, gliding across the room. Her new emerald green wool skirts swished enticingly with each step. "Please don't do any more for me, David. It's too much." There was a quiver in her voice she was unable to hide.

"Why, darling!" He reached for her and drew her into

his arms. "What is wrong? Surely, my gifts alone cannot be the cause of such intense distress."

"But they are!" she cried, throwing her arms around his neck. "Please understand I am grateful for your generosity. It is so kindly meant that I adore you for it a thousand times over. But it also makes me feel guilty, at times."

"Guilty!" He looked astonished. "Whatever for? You've done nothing wrong, and neither have I."

"No, of course not! It's just that…" She paused and nibbled on her lower lip. "It's difficult to have it so good as your wife, while my mother and sisters are barely making ends meet. It doesn't seem right to acquire another dress or hat or even a book, when they might not be certain of their next meal. I know, I know," she moaned at his expression. "I'm being difficult again. But you've confessed several times that you knew you were marrying a sassy southern wench, so there you have it."

He swayed back and forth with her in a slow dance. "Perhaps it will ease the mind of my sassy southern wench to learn that her — what is it you've called me so many times? Ah, yes. Her quiet, brooding husband, not that I have had the luxury of being very quiet since I married you, nor do I have ample time in which to properly brood, any longer." He bent his head to capture her mouth in a long and satisfying kiss. "That said, this formerly brooding fellow sent a cheque to your mother the same day you composed your last letter to her. I assure you, my darling wife, that it is enough to cover her rent and groceries for a year with enough left over to commission a gown or two."

She was so overcome with amazement that she fisted her hands in his silk dinner jacket. "You did? Oh, David! How can I ever thank you?"

He waggled his brows at her. "I can think of one very pleasurable way."

She used her grip on his jacket to yank him closer. "You're a cad!"

"A cad for you, darling." He dove in for another kiss.

She kissed him back, pouring her heart to him through her lips. It was a very long time before either recovered their ability to converse. By then, neither of them could recall the original topic.

Throughout the last few cold days of November and the even colder days of December, they continued their daily drives to the home they were building. When the snow got too deep to drag their carriage through it, David purchased a sleigh and took his bride on a sleigh ride each afternoon.

Elizabeth wasn't sure how her husband did it, but he managed to recruit construction teams from several neighboring towns. The result was, their home was completed in record time, despite the weather — one whole week before Christmas.

Chapter 7: Unexpected Visitor

ELLIZABETH

W idow Gable insisted on bundling up like an Eskimo and accompanying Elizabeth and David on several of the trips to their new home. Elizabeth tried to talk her into staying at Rose Haven where it was warm, but the woman insisted she was as much a part of their move as anyone since she'd stored Elizabeth's trunks for free all this time.

Elizabeth didn't have the heart to turn down her assistance, realizing — like a mother or grandmother — she truly wanted to be a part of this special occasion in their lives. Elizabeth smiled indulgently as Widow Gable puttered around the two stories of their new home, making recommendations for furnishings and decorations.

"We have more crystal, linens, and paintings than you can shake a stick at," Elizabeth bemoaned to her. "What we have precious little of is furniture."

"Well, I happen to have more than I can use," Widow Gable returned tartly. "I'll have Sam rustle up a team of men to pay a visit to my home at the end of Main Street.

Just tell me what you want, and I'll have it delivered. Today, if you wish."

"You have a home down on Main?" Elizabeth was astonished. "I reckon I was under the impression you resided at Rose Haven."

"I do," the woman returned matter-of-factly, "which is exactly why I have more furniture than I need." She smoothed her hands down her pristine white apron. "Since I couldn't bear to part with a thing after Matthew died, I more or less boarded up our townhome and left everything the way it was. I haven't hardly stepped foot inside it for more than a year, other than to air it out now and then and ensure no families of mice were trying to take up residence there."

Elizabeth was amazed. "I appreciate your kindness and generosity so very much, but I couldn't possibly help myself to your things like that. It wouldn't be right."

"Why not?" Widow Gable stuck out her bony chin. "I figure it's mine to do whatever I want with, and it's you I want to have it."

"But—"

"No but's," she interrupted sharply. "You're like the daughter I never had, and David is equally dear to me. Why, even that rascal, Sam Bullock, has worn down the soft part of my nerves."

"I don't know," Elizabeth sighed. She couldn't bear the thought of being accused of taking advantage of the elder woman's generosity. She'd already done so much for her and David — too much.

"Well, I *do* know, and my mind is quite made up." The widow nodded sharply. "Here's an idea, though. If David fusses louder than you over what I'm about to do with my furniture, tell him he can fund the ingredients for that stew I like to deliver to the chaps at the livery. He can fund my hobby for as long as he likes. I enjoy feeding hungry men, but I can't afford to do it for free as often as I'd prefer. I've a tab at the mercantile. Lord knows Wallace Weston could use the business, what with a wife and his brood of five youngsters to feed."

Elizabeth nodded happily. That sounded like something her kindhearted husband would be delighted to agree to. Her worries appeased, she had Sam drive her and Widow Gable to the woman's townhome, which happened to be up a secluded drive off the beaten path of Main Street. It was no ordinary townhome, either. It turned out to be a few bricks shy of a mansion.

"Oh, my!" she exclaimed when she saw the beautiful home. It was three stories of red and white stone with more windows and balconies than a person could shake a stick at. "It's a veritable castle."

"It is," the widow agreed grimly. "Way too large for one old woman to be rattling around in alone. I should have sold it months ago."

"It's your home!" Elizabeth protested.

"Bah!" the elder woman slapped at the air with one gloved hand. "Home is right here, my dear." She pointed at her heart. "And the memories stay up top." She tapped her temple. "The rest is just stuff."

The things she called *just stuff* turned out to be an ornate dining room set with hand carved legs and claw feet, a collection of antique armoires and dressers, two four-poster beds, so many tables and basins that Elizabeth lost count of them, Persian rugs, velvet sofas, an array of armchairs, and — marvel of marvels — a pianoforte.

"It's too much," she gasped. "I can't possibly take it all home." It would take years, more years than Widow Gable had left, for David to fund enough stew ingredients to cover the cost of purchasing so much furniture, and such grand pieces at that.

"You can and you will," her friend returned tartly. "These are my things to give. If it's any comfort, I'll take the liberty of inviting myself over as often as I like to sit in my former chairs and eat at my former table. Does that sound fair enough?"

"Oh, please do!" Her voice choked with emotion, Elizabeth threw her arms around the tiny woman and gave her a fierce hug. "Your things are so beautiful. Even if I had unlimited funds and time to travel the entire world, I wouldn't be able to find furniture that would make me any happier than this."

"How else do you think I acquired so much?" the woman cackled. She held Elizabeth at an arm's length. "That's exactly what Matthew and I did. He owned an international shipping business, so we traveled the world until we were too old to do it any longer. Then we ended up back here, not far from where we grew up. It pleased him to no end to make building a new town his final mission. He was happy here. *We* were happy here, just as you and David will be."

"We already are," Elizabeth sighed. "I feel like Cinderella. A penniless girl who married a real prince of a man."

"That you did, dearie, and don't you forget that in the coming months."

"Whatever do you mean?" She was startled by the woman's sudden change of tone.

But Widow Gable merely pressed her lips together.

"Mrs. Gable, if you know something that you need to tell me…"

"I don't," she snapped, "or I shouldn't. Ah, fiddle-sticks!" She waved both gloved hands. "I can't say more without betraying a confidence, but I meant what I said. David is the man for you, doll. Don't you ever forget it, you hear?"

"Of course he is!" she sputtered. "I'm so in love with him I can't see straight most days."

"Indeed? Well, that besotted man hasn't seen straight since the day you stepped off your stagecoach."

Elizabeth impulsively reached for her hands. "Please, Mrs. Gable. Is there something I should be worried about? You are starting to make me think there is."

The elder woman made a face. "Not so long as you guard his heart, sweet girl. That man loves you so much, it's downright terrifying. Takes insult after insult on the nose from the locals about his choice of investments during the war, all the while he's working to help rebuild the rail system in Atlanta."

Elizabeth gasped. "My husband is doing what?" she shouted, dropping the widow's hands. How could she not have known this?

"Bah!" Her companion grimaced. "I've gone and said too much. I believe it was supposed to be a surprise. Alas, the news hit one of the gazettes a few towns over. I know folks." She nodded smartly. "I know folks who know other folks, and word gets back to me about, well, most everything."

Elizabeth chuckled. She couldn't help it, since Widow Gable seemed to be operating her own little spy network. "I'll keep your secret and act surprised when he gets around to telling me."

They shared a hearty laugh.

"See?" Widow Gable stabbed the air in her direction with one finger. "You might as well have been my daughter. You think just like me."

E lizabeth enjoyed every minute of the festivities leading up to Christmas in Angel Creek. There was the tree lighting in the town square followed by their annual chili cook-off, sponsored by the ladies auxiliary. Then there were the shop windows on Main that no longer looked so weathered and homely with pine bows and red ribbons showing through the glass panes.

David was impressed with all the stately furniture Widow Gable sent over to grace their new home. "I had no idea she was hoarding so many beautiful things, or I would have offered to buy them off of her weeks ago," he declared.

Elizabeth filled him in on the widow's request to start a regular dinner fund for the hardworking fellows over at the livery.

"Consider it done." He bent to kiss her full on the lips in sight of the workmen who happened to be delivering furniture.

"David!" she hissed, blushing.

He pretended puzzlement, but his dark eyes glinted knowingly. He dodged the hand she swatted at his shoulder and left the dining room, whistling merrily, to direct the movers where to place the pianoforte they'd been gifted.

Sam muttered threats beneath his breath the entire time he was carting tables and chairs inside. Elizabeth suspected he'd have a few choice words for the boarding house proprietress the next time he saw her.

When the moving crew was nearly finished delivering their new furniture, Widow Gable set herself to helping dress the beds with linens and the windows with curtains.

"You've got to get back to Rose Haven," Elizabeth

chided. "You've already worked your fingers close enough to the bone for one day."

"Nonsense," the woman countered and continued setting their bedroom to rights.

As the afternoon ripened to evening, the boarding house proprietress constantly seemed to be peeking out the front windows. Elizabeth began to suspect something might be amiss. Nothing good, from the deepening scowl on Widow Gable's lined features.

David returned from a trip to the mercantile with Sam and offered to drive her back to the boarding house, but she pooh-poohed his suggestion as well.

"There's plenty of work to be done still. Sam can take me back at nightfall when there's no more light left to work."

Sam left the room, hands in the pockets of his overalls, grumbling under his breath some more.

As the dinner hour approached, Widow Gable moved to the kitchen and helped herself to the pots and pans David had purchased from the mercantile earlier, as well as the stack of groceries he'd acquired. In little time, she had a pot of chicken and dumplings simmering on the stove.

But before they could take their seats around their newly acquired dining room table, the sound of sleigh bells filled the air.

Elizabeth's mystified gaze met David's equally mystified gaze across the room. They'd not been expecting company.

"I'll get the door," he said simply.

"I'll go with you." She smiled sweetly up at him. "Methinks it would be fitting to greet our first visitor together."

He stooped to nuzzle noses with her. When he straightened, she couldn't help admiring how handsome he was in his white linen shirt and black and gray striped waistcoat.

"Keep looking at me like that, wife, and it'll be a long time before we make it to the front door," he warned.

She rolled her eyes and swept past him, beating him to the foyer

At the last second, his hand covered hers on the knob, and they opened the door together.

All she could do was blink and stare for a full minute. "Charley?" she finally managed to gasp out.

Chapter 8: The Choice

ELIZABETH

All Elizabeth could do was blink and stare for a full minute. "Charley?" she finally managed to gasp out again.

He was much different from the man she remembered. Taller, for one thing, a good two inches or more, and terribly gaunt. His cheeks were pale and sunken, and the angles and planes of his face more pronounced than she remembered. His overcoat hung on him as if it was many times too large.

"Come in, soldier," David invited in the habitually calm and quiet tones in which he greeted everyone around town.

"It's Lieutenant Arrington to you, sir." Charley stormed inside the foyer, with the help of a walking stick. He moved with a limp, practically dragging one leg behind him.

"Why, Charley!" Elizabeth reprimanded. "What an awful way to greet the husband of an old friend!"

"Old friend, eh?" He glared down at her, with snow dripping from his auburn lashes.

She folded her arms and stared angrily back at him. "A very dear friend," she reiterated firmly.

"Here and I thought you were my affianced all that time," he growled.

"I'm a married woman now," she reminded, tapping one of the toes of her new black boots. "I'll thank you to remember it, else I'll toss you back out in the snow. See if I won't!"

They stared each other down for several tense moments.

He finally broke into a grin. "Lord have mercy, but I've missed you, Liz!" His hazel eyes glinted with unshed tears; but for all she could tell, they were happy ones. Without warning, he enveloped her in a bear hug. "I had to come see for myself that you were content with your decision to stay married to this bloke." He took a step back and stabbed the air with his walking stick in David's direction.

"Charley," she warned.

"Alas, I see that you are," he continued in a mournful voice. "More's the pity for me."

"I'm sorry for all you suffered. I truly am," she said quickly. "And I am more thankful than words can express that you are alive."

"But…" he prodded, angling his head in David's direction.

"But I love my husband very much."

"I can see that, too," he sighed. His shoulders relaxed, and he caught David's eye over her head. "Keep her happy, sir, or this is one southern boy you won't want to face, despite my baggy pants and walking stick."

David nodded. "I plan to."

Elizabeth's head waved back and forth between them, until she could assure herself no shots were about to be fired.

"I loved her first, and I will always love her," Charley announced in an emphatic tone. "You'll just have to live with that, too."

"Fair enough, soldier." David waved a hand at the dining room table, looking none perturbed for the bite in the younger man's voice. "Seeing as I'm not likely to rid myself of you any time soon, would you care to join us for dinner?"

"I would." He nodded at Elizabeth and took his place by her side.

Elizabeth moaned inside her head at the notion of attempting to eat dinner at the same table as her husband and her former affianced. She caught David's eye and sent him a pleading look. In the process of pulling out her chair for her, he managed to speak softly in her ear. "It's alright, love. I can share you for an hour." He nipped at her earlobe. "So long as you kiss me with your eyes every time you look in my direction." With that outrageous statement, he took his seat at the head of the table, close enough to reach under the table and give her hand a reassuring squeeze.

Widow Gable breezed into the room with her pot of dumplings. "I couldn't help overhearing some of what you said, young man." This she directed at Charley. "Figured I'd let you know I'm single again. The finest woman in town might be taken by the dashing captain, but the second finest woman is recently widowed."

After a moment of shocked silence, both Charley and David burst out laughing. The tension in the room was lessened.

Long before they finished eating, the sound of sleigh bells filled the air again.

Elizabeth froze in her seat.

Charley patted her shoulder. "Do not fret, beautiful.

I'm the only old flame who'll be paying you a visit this evening. The others pulling up to your front porch are welcome guests, indeed. I simply asked them to give me a running start in the event I could talk you into coming home."

"This is my home," she said firmly. Then it dawned on her who he was speaking about. "Oh, Charley! You didn't!" She leaped to her feet so quickly, she nearly knocked over her chair.

Both gentlemen shot to their feet, as well.

"Oh, but I did, beautiful."

With a shriek of unladylike delight, she sprinted for the front door — not quickly enough, as it turned out, to miss hearing her two favorite men in the world snarl at each other.

"Her name is Elizabeth," David announced coolly. "Not beautiful or doll or sugar or honey. You'll either call her by her given name, or you'll be addressing her as Mrs. Pemberton from now on."

"Aye, aye, captain."

Elizabeth glanced over her shoulder in time to catch Charley's mock salute. Rolling her eyes, she flung open the front door for the second time that evening. "Mama!" she cried. "Grace, Lilly, and Mags!" Her youngest sister was named Magnolia, but they'd referred to her as Mags ever since she was a tiny thing, because she was forever pilfering through Mama's collection of magazines.

The four women bustled laughing and crying through the front door and launched themselves at Elizabeth in a rainbow of coats, hats, muffs, and dresses. All the girls were blonde like their oldest sister. Their mother, who used to be blonde, was now a salt and pepper version of it.

Someone must have shut the front door for them, because the icy breeze halted after a few seconds.

Grace, who was only a year younger, managed to wedge her way directly in front of her oldest sister. She gripped her shoulders and shook her. "Pray assure me things are solidly over between you and Charley," she hissed. "No more understandings of any sort."

Lilly, who was nineteen, shoved Grace out of the way to wrap Elizabeth in a tight hug. "Or she'll have to scratch your eyes out." She stepped back and addressed Grace squarely. "We get it, sugar. You always did wear your heart on your sleeve for the—"

"Lilly!" Grace blurted with a distressed glance in the direction of the dining room where Charley and David were watching them in utmost bemusement.

"Mags, honey!" Elizabeth curled an arm around their youngest sister's shoulders. She was but seventeen. "I'm so glad you decided to visit me for Christmas."

"It was all Charley's doing, precious," their mother assured with a simpering smile in his direction. "He knew there was nothing you'd want more for the holidays than a visit from your family."

"He was right." Elizabeth regarded them with brimming eyes. "I'm so overcome I hardly know what to say." She dabbed at her eyes with the backs of her hands.

"Oh, dear heavens!" Her mother produced a clean white handkerchief and pressed it in her hand. "Where's your hankie, doll? I thought I raised you better."

"You did," Elizabeth assured. "Pray forgive my lapse in manners, Mama dearest." She dabbed at her damp cheeks with the cloth.

"So you're the lovely mother who raised this lovely daughter." Widow Gable, who'd been standing by the front door all this time, stepped forward and held out her hands to Mrs. Byrd.

"I am," Miranda Byrd declared proudly. "Thank you for including me in your kind words. And you are?"

"Her foster mother, I reckon, in your absence." Widow Gable grinned. "But I'm happy to step back into the position of a grandmother or a favorite aunt now that you've arrived to town. How long will you be staying?" she inquired pertly.

After eyeing the fuzzy haired older woman a moment, Miranda's gaze softened. The spritely widow was simply one of those women who was impossible not to adore at first sight. "I haven't the slightest idea," she confessed with a rueful glance in Charley's direction. "We risked freezing ourselves to death traveling this time of year, though we were highly motivated by the thought of seeing Liz again. I'm afraid, we won't be so motivated on the return trip," she sighed.

"Then it's decided." Widow Gable clapped her hands. "You'll remain in Angel Creek until the spring thaw. I've the perfect place in mind for you and the girls to stay."

Elizabeth's lips parted in amazement. Did Martha Gable mean what she thought she meant? She sent the woman a questioning look.

The widow winked merrily at her. "Though you might be sleeping on cots for a few days. Elizabeth nigh on cleaned me out of furniture earlier today."

Elizabeth gaped at her. *It was all your idea!*

"Not to worry, however. I've a warehouse on the edge of town crammed so full of treasures, there's hardly room enough to step between them to explore it all."

You own a warehouse, too? "Of course you do," Elizabeth murmured faintly. Eventually, she expected to learn that the widow actually owned the entire town or was related to a foreign prince or some other exotic nonsense. "Say yes, Mama," she urged.

"To what?" Mrs. Byrd arched one regal brow at her oldest daughter.

"Just say yes. Trust me."

"Oo, a pianoforte!" Lilly stepped into the parlor to run her fingers lovingly over the keys. "'I heard the bells on Christmas day,'" she sang sweetly.

A hush settled over those gathered.

She continued singing. "'Their old familiar carols play. And wild and sweet the words repeat. Of peace on earth, good will to men.'"

Written by Henry Wadsworth Longfellow during the Civil War, the lyrics echoed the man's personal tragedies as well as those of a nation divided by wounds almost too deep for words.

And thought how, as the day had come,
The belfries of all Christendom
Had rolled along the unbroken song
Of peace on earth, good will to men.

Till ringing, singing on its way
The world revolved from night to day,
A voice, a chime, a chant sublime
Of peace on earth, good will to men.

Then from each black, accursed mouth
The cannon thundered in the South, And with the
*   sound*
The carols drowned
Of peace on earth, good-will to men!

It was as if an earthquake rent
The hearth-stones of a continent,
And made forlorn The households born

Of peace on earth, good-will to men!

And in despair I bowed my head
"There is no peace on earth," I said,
"For hate is strong and mocks the song
Of peace on earth, good will to men."

Then pealed the bells more loud and deep:
"God is not dead, nor doth He sleep;
The wrong shall fail, the right prevail
With peace on earth, good will to men.

W hen Lilly finished trilling out the last line of the beautiful carol, there was hardly a dry eye in Elizabeth and David's new home. Dabbing at his eyes with a much-wrinkled piece of cloth, Sam tromped his way down the second story stairs in his work boots.

"I thought I heard an angel chorus," he muttered gruffly. "Looks like I was right."

"Why, thank you, dear fellow." Lilly nodded at Mags. Their youngest sister took over the pianoforte and launched into a much merrier carol, Deck the Halls, while Lilly curtsied in front of Sam.

"May I have this dance, sir?"

"What, ho?" He looked startled at first, then mightily pleased when she reached for his callused hand and twirled in a pirouette beneath it. Her mauve skirts billowed out, swishing against the legs of his overalls.

The moment Mags finished playing Deck the Halls, she launched into the equally merry tune, Up on the Housetop.

David sauntered across the foyer and swung Elizabeth

into a dance. They twirled, dipped, and swayed beneath the flickering candles of the crystal chandelier Widow Gable had insisted they take from her townhome. A few steps away, a fire leaped in the hearth of stacked stone, bringing welcome heat and more light into the room.

After a moment of wry hesitation, Charley shuffled his way in the direction of the merriment. Grace was the only other young person standing and watching.

He rested his walking stick against the wide doorway and crooked an elbow at her.

Color rising in her fair cheeks, she glided gracefully in his direction.

Elizabeth watched them from the corner of her eye, wondering if Charley noted her sister's besotted expression. Poor Grace! It was tough holding a candle for a man who only had eyes for another. Then again, Charley had taken the news of her marriage better than she expected. Maybe there was hope for his full recovery after all — body, heart, and spirit.

David bent his head to bring them to eye level. "Is all well with my wife tonight?"

She gave him a joyous smile. "'God is in his Heaven. All's right with the world,'" she answered softly. It was a quote from a poem by Robert Browning.

"All's more than right with my world," David agreed. His gaze burned passionately into hers. "So long as you are in it, love."

"Oh, I intend to be in it for a very long time," she assured, standing on her tiptoes to brush her lips against his. "You've been warned." She dared not look at her mother. The poor woman was probably having an apoplectic fit over her oldest daughter's second public lapse in propriety that evening. But she could worry about her mama's sensitivities later. The only thing that mattered at the moment was reassuring David of her love and devotion to him. It had to have been a trying evening, opening the door and coming face-to-face with her formerly dead affianced.

That would be a tale to tell their grandchildren some day, for sure!

Epilogue

T he spring thaw brought the blooms back to Angel Creek, but the trees and flowers weren't the only thing blooming. Elizabeth's belly swelled with child.

"First a library. Now a nursery. You sure know how to keep a man busy," David grumbled good-naturedly. He'd just returned from another trip to California where he'd met with a set of new investors. He cuddled her close and kissed her hungrily.

She kissed him back but had her nose nicely wrinkled when he gave her a moment to breathe again. "I hope our son kicks you good and hard for that jibe." She pressed her blooming middle against him.

He chuckled exultantly and splayed his large hands against the sides of her belly. "Kick away, little tiger. Your daddy's ready."

"I hope you're equally ready to escort me to the town picnic this afternoon." Elizabeth fluttered her lashes at him. "I've a new hat to show off and nowhere else to show it off to, if you're not willing to oblige me."

He snorted. "By all means, put me to work the moment I walk through the door."

"It's a picnic, not work," she assured saucily.

"Huh! Says you. I'll need to fortify myself first." He sealed his mouth over hers for another fiercely tender kiss. "You're not the one who'll be facing down the barrel of the anti-David Pemberton club members."

"What? I'm quite sure Caroline forgave you eons ago," she protested. "Lilly explained it all to her in a letter before her arrival, how you've been helping rebuild the rail lines in Atlanta."

"Hm, then there must be another reason she stares daggers at me every time we meet."

"Maybe she's just admiring your brawny self," Elizabeth teased, but she knew better. Poor Caroline hadn't been a big fan of David to begin with. But after Charley's arrival into town, she'd been even less of a fan, bemoaning her own foolishness at every opportunity for talking Elizabeth into becoming a mail-order bride.

The afternoon at the town picnic was no exception.

She managed to corner Elizabeth at the lemonade stand. "If I'd had any idea Charley was still alive," she wailed, fanning her face and looking mournfully in his direction.

He was standing just outside a copse of dogwoods, Lilly and Grace were chatting with him. Well, Lilly was, anyway. Most folks didn't get too many words in when she was present. Charley was watching her with amusement. Grace was watching Charley with thinly concealed adoration.

"If that were the case, then Grace would have never forgiven either of us." Elizabeth finished merrily. "My sister has adored that man to distraction for as long as I can remember. I always did feel a bit guilty about courting Charley, knowing how she felt about him."

"Stuff and nonsense!" Caroline protested. "He always did belong to you, one hundred percent."

Elizabeth shook her head. "There were times I seriously had to wonder if she loved him more than I did. I think I've since discovered the answer to that."

"He will always love you," her friend insisted. "You can see it every time he looks at you."

"And I will always love him, in return." She pressed her palms to her belly. "Just not the way he wants or deserves, because I love my husband more. So much that it scares me sometimes, Caro."

"I don't know what you see in him. I really don't." Caroline waved away a bee buzzing nearby.

"He's helping rebuild Atlanta," she reminded a little more sharply than she intended.

"I know, E."

"He's been taking care of Mama and my sisters."

"So Lilly claims." Her friend pursed her lips.

"Plus, he's wildly handsome," Elizabeth teased. "Deny it all you want, but we both know it's true."

"Don't press your luck, sweetie." Her friend giggled. "I'm already married to the brawniest man in the west, remember?"

Elizabeth smiled, not the least offended by her friend's bragging. She was just glad Caroline and Adam had found happiness together. Just as David Pemberton was her own perfect match. She was convinced of it, despite all of Caroline's humorous shenanigans to the contrary.

She glanced across the grassy plain surrounding the town square and caught her husband's eyes on her.

I love you, she mouthed.

I love you, too, he mouthed back.

Yes. He was the perfect man for her. 'Til the end of her days.

<<< THE END >>>

I hope you enjoyed this story! The next book in this series is...

Emma

Emma Bowen and her friends have lost nearly everything to the war and starting over has been almost impossible for the Charleston women. So, when their friend, Caroline, received an encouraging letter from Julia Bailey offering a solution to their problems, they all jumped at the chance to leave the ravages of war behind.

Colin Cassidy, former Union Army captain, was reported killed in battle more than a year ago. And after what he has done, he'd rather let everyone go on thinking him dead. He'd rather spend the rest of his worthless life numbing his guilt at the bottom of a whiskey bottle than have his family learn the truth about what he's done. But when his brother, Quinn, shows up on his doorstep, he kidnaps Colin and forces him to spend Christmas in Angel Creek, Montana.

Emma desperately needs to find a purpose for her life. Colin doesn't want a life at all. Can a Christmas miracle bring two enemies together through one more Christmas miracle?

To find out more, check out our Amazon Series Page. Then keep turning to read a few sneak previews. Much love, Jo

---

Angel Cookie
Christmas

JO
GRAFFORD

Pinetop Homecoming

A knock sounded at the front door of Willa Murray's townhouse. She jolted from her stance in front of the flickering fire and set her mug of hot tea on the white-washed oak mantle above the hearth. She'd been using it to her warm her icy fingers. It had miserably failed to chase away the cold ache in her heart.

Though the nightlife in Tombstone, Arizona was in full swing at nine o' clock, it was a fairly late hour for visitors. Frowning at the interruption of her trip down melancholy lane, she smoothed her hands over the full skirts of her purple velvet theater gown, forced a smile fit for the stage, and glided to the entry foyer. Her high-heeled boots clicked against the black and white marble tiles, echoing down the shadowy hall.

She cautiously peered through the peephole but could see no movement on the other side of the door. No person, no animal, nothing except the ghostly, swirling leaves from the trio of dying mountain laurels forming a soldierly straight line on her lawn. They provided the only nod to privacy between her front door and the busy city street beyond it.

Mystified, she threw the deadbolt and slid the door open a crack. A mid-November breeze whistled through the opening, making her shiver. Glancing across her empty covered portico, she was about to close the door when a small square package caught her eye.

From the glow of street lanterns, she could see it was wrapped in plain brown parchment paper with a bow of thin string securing it. *What now?* Accustomed to the fawning attention of adoring fans and an occasional stalker, she pushed the door open wider and threw another glance around the empty yard and portico before venturing onto the cobblestone walkway. She snatched up the small gift and hurried back inside with it clutched to her chest. She firmly shut the door and stood, panting and blinking back tears, with her shoulder blades pressed against its heavy wood paneling.

Harlan Stoneriver, may he rest in peace, had been fond of leaving her whimsical and impromptu gifts all seasons of the year and all hours of the day and night. But the odd little package couldn't be from him unless the ghost of his Christmas past had scheduled an early holiday appearance. The truth was Harlan Stoneriver was never going to deliver her another half-limp cluster of wildflowers or quirky piece of pottery, because he'd died in a riding accident. Today was the four month anniversary of his tragic passing.

"What am I going to do without you?" she wailed to the empty foyer, letting her tears flow freely now that she was safely inside the walls of her luxurious home once more. "Best friends don't leave best friends alone in the world like this. They just...don't."

He'd been her boss, her mentor, the owner of the thriving theater company she worked for. And now that he was gone, his younger brother had taken over — a man whose knowledge about the acting business wouldn't fill a teacup. A man who couldn't be bothered with trivial things like patron attendance records or ticket sales. He was too busy flirting with the female cast members, indulging himself in Harlan's collection of fine wines from around the world, and installing his favorite niece as the next darling of Desert Productions.

Maybe if Willa had flirted back, he wouldn't be working so hard to replace her. A familiar feeling of revulsion washed over her, staunching her tears. Over her dead body would that slimy excuse of a man paw her face or figure! If he were the last marriageable man on earth, she would choose a life of spinsterhood over him, no jest.

A prospect that was becoming more and more likely with her twenty-eighth birthday approaching and the closest thing she'd ever had to a beau resting beneath the frosty ground in Tombstone Cemetery…

Blowing a few loose strands of dark hair from her damp cheeks, she took a closer look at the package. A tiny card was threaded through the bow of string. Opening it, she was amazed at how spidery the signature appeared, as if someone very old had written it. Someone very old and very spicy from the heady scent of ginger and molasses wafting up from the paper.

She read the name, squinted at the smudged ink, then read it again. If her eyesight was to be trusted, the letter was from the North Pole! *Unbelievable! Someone had to be playing a prank on her.* It was from Mrs. Claus, to be exact, and it read:

Watch for the angel in disguise who will soon cross your path.

What a puzzling message! Thoroughly intrigued, Willa tore open the small package, dropped the paper to the floor, and stared at the delicate box cupped in her hands. It was white cardboard with an intricate eyelet snowflake pattern cut into each side. Whoever had sent it possessed a lovely eye for gift packaging. She lifted the fragile lid and gasped.

An iced gingerbread cookie ornament in the shape of an angel lay inside, nestled on a bed of snowy white felt. She lifted the box to breathe in the soothing aroma of gingerbread and holiday spices, and her heavy heart instantly lifted a few degrees.

Thank you, Mrs. Claus or whoever you are. I really needed a dose of holiday magic this evening.

She sashayed her way back to the parlor and ever so gently propped the precious gift on her mantle. It leaned against the wall like a delicious morsel of hope drizzled in white icing. She reached for her mug, only to carry it to the kitchen and dump the remaining contents in the sink. Her fingers were no longer cold.

She retired to her bed chamber, where her part-time maid had so thoughtfully drawn her a steamy bath. *You're an angel, Tilly, if I ever met one! Not one in disguise, though.* She bathed, changed into her white silk night robe, and lounged against the mountain of quilted lilac pillows on her antique four-poster bed. An hour later, she was still wide awake, unable to get the angel cookie ornament out of her mind.

Gingerbread always reminded her of Christmastime and home. Home was Pinetop, Arizona, a small town she hadn't visited near often enough since her launch to stardom. Her acting career had taken her to theaters all over the world the past ten years. Sure, she tried to squeeze in a quick visit home now and then, but Christmas? The last time she'd been home for Christmas was...

Ugh! She sat up and rubbed her eyes, making her down-filled mattress puff up a bit around her legs. It had been so long she was having trouble pinpointing the exact time. Six years? Maybe seven? Too long.

I really should go visit my folks. Mother and Father would be overjoyed to spend the holidays with their only child.

She stared across her enormous moonlit chamber and allowed the endless months of loneliness and homesickness wash over her. She certainly had the time for a visit home this holiday season. Thanks to the new owner of Desert Productions replacing her lead role in the upcoming Christmas play with his niece, she had the next several weeks to do whatever she wished. She wasn't scheduled to work again until January.

Yes, indeed, it was time for a visit home — not one of those rushed stopovers between productions either. A real visit. The several week kind.

Her mind made up, Willa plopped back on her pile of pillows, scattering several across the bed. One dropped to the wood floor with a soft, muted thud, and she was finally able to fall sleep.

S he rose at dawn, attempted to throw together a quick travel bag, and gave up in defeat. She simply didn't possess the ability to pack quickly or lightly. She might be staying in Pinetop for six weeks or longer. That required some careful planning when it came to her gown selection, shoes and accessories, toiletries, and comfort items like scented candles, books, and that spare theater prop or two a girl never knew she needed until she did.

She was surrounded by mountains of hat boxes and shoes by the time her maid made her morning appearance.

"Land sakes, child!" Tilly Cassidy took one look at the towering piles of female belongings, smoothed her white ruffled work cap farther back on her pile of red hair, and dove in to set the room to rights.

Her mother hen attitude never failed to amuse Willa, considering she was a good five to six years younger than her employer.

Regardless, her maid had the chaos sorted and her mistress ready for the road in a half hour sharp. "There now, love. My cousin, Paul, can drive you to the train station. He'll be here shortly to fetch me like he always does, and the station is right on our way to the Rileys."

Willa could tell by the young woman's slight grimace that she wasn't looking forward to her daily grind at the Riley mansion, and no wonder. Their four stair-step daughters she was attempting to teach needle point weren't exactly the best behaved little poppets.

She spun around to her oval dressing mirror to pat a stray dark ringlet back in place. Then she tipped her wide-brimmed, navy felt travel hat to a sassier angle. Large bonnets were the rage these days, but Willa possessed a style of her own. A hat was what she was in the mood to wear home, so a hat was what she was wearing. It had been custom designed for a part she'd played recently on stage as a vigilante. It was a wee bit on the roguish side, which made her adore it all the more.

Most of her gowns were also specially commissioned, and today's travel gown was no exception. It was a military cut with severe, straight gathers that ran down her blue brocade bodice and ended in a point just above the flair of her full skirts. She couldn't abide the enormous bell-shaped skirts that made it impossible to sit comfortably or move around freely without bumping into something, so she wore a single petticoat beneath her travel gown. She never used fashion as an excuse to torture her naturally slender frame with whale-boned bodices or tight corsets like so many other women did.

"Here you go, love." Tilly held out a double breasted gray frock coat with shiny gold buttons. Her heart-shaped features were squished into an I-don't-understand expression, but she was too polite to comment on her mistress's choice of jackets.

"Thank you." Willa smothered a chuckle, knowing her maid much preferred to see her in frilly princess-style ball-gowns and cloaks. She shrugged on the coat then spun around to bid a silent goodbye to her spacious bed chamber. Even though her parents were well off, they didn't own a residence nearly as sumptuous as hers. She would dearly miss the extra space. Her old bedroom, where she would be staying in Pinetop, was less than half the size of this one. Instead of six wardrobes lined end to end, she would have to fit the contents of her many travel bags into one. There would be no lounge on the side of her old room either, no private claw-foot tub behind an Oriental screen, and no maid to spoil her.

Which reminded her…

Sighing, she reached for the long white envelope resting on the edge of her roll-top writing desk. "I have a little something for you before I go." It was the first item of business she'd attended after waking.

Tilly tore into the envelope with the gusto of a small child opening a gift on Christmas morning. "Why, Miss Willa!" Her eyes bulged with excitement. "I don't understand."

"It's your next six weeks of wages," she explained softly. "I'll not be having you replace me with another family while I'm out of town."

"You know I would n-never…" Tilly's lips began to tremble. "I'm sorry, but I can't accept this. It wouldn't be right, since I didn't earn it." She tried to hand the envelope back, but Willa could see what it cost her. Her normally clear gray eyes locked on the money and took on a desperate tinge. It was obvious she needed the funds.

Not for the first time, Willa burned with curiosity about her mysterious, well-spoken maid. How a woman of her obvious culture and breeding came to be in the service of others in the first place… "It's a gift, my friend. You don't need to earn gifts. If it makes you feel any better, I am likely to return from Pinetop with a mountain of mending to tend, which means you'll be putting in extra hours soon enough. You know how hard I can be on my dresses at times."

With a moan of surrender, Tilly launched herself at her mistress, throwing her arms around her and squeezing her tight. "Thank you from the bottom of my heart."

A fist pounded on the front door.

"That'll be Paul." She dropped her arms and dabbed at her eyes.

She looked so forlorn standing there in her simple gray work dress and white ruffled apron that Willa's heart went out to her. "Maybe you can visit Pinetop with me some day."

Her maid gave her a sad smile. They both knew she wasn't at liberty to take off work whenever she pleased. Families like the Rileys would let her go in a heartbeat if she tried.

"Maybe some day," she agreed softly.

From the window of her private train car, Willa watched the overcrowded streets of Tombstone disappear. She'd never noticed it before but the lone schoolhouse and ice cream parlor almost seemed to be swallowed up by the endless rows of saloons and gambling halls. Even the Desert Dreams Theater where she worked looked a wee bit dismal on a Saturday morning. The front doors were locked, its enormous chandeliers of newfangled incandescent lightbulbs were quenched, and the wide columned portico was empty of carriages dropping off and picking up guests.

Too excited to nap, she drank in the arid scenery flying past her windows — miles of sand dunes tinged pink by the morning sun, clusters of palo verde trees stripped naked by the cooler temperatures of late autumn, and towering rosy ridges and mesas.

It took nearly four hours of northward travel for the desert terrain to transition to the cooler plateaus of the highland region. Up here, the countryside was punctuated by mountain ranges and scattered forests.

Pinetop was nestled atop one of the lower lying mountains, hidden from the surrounding deserts by junipers, firs, and pines. Willa's excitement rose several notches as the train slowed and began its final ascent to her hometown. It was a mid-sized town, not near as big as Tombstone but a far cry from rural. There was no place in the world quite like it.

Growing up there had been like being immersed in Christmas magic year-round. Main Street was dotted with festive storefronts. Their wide picture windows boasted fresh baked goods, hand-spun candies, sweet and spicy meats, festive hats, fancy shoes and boots, fashionable dresses and smart business suits, a watch maker and clock repairman as ancient as Santa himself, a semi-famous dog breeder advertising cuddly adoptions, and dozens more fascinating and alluring goods and services. Citizens travelled here from all over the state to shop and vacation, but even more so during the holidays.

As the first city street rolled into view, nostalgia clogged Willa's throat. In Pinetop, she'd had everything a child could dream up — two adoring indulgent parents, a gingerbread-like two-story chalet, mountains of toys, private singing and dancing lessons, a nanny-turned-companion as she grew older, and a circle of friends from the town's most elite citizens. Bankers' children, attorneys' children, the mayor's son and daughter. All of whom were long-since married to other well bred and highly accomplished young men and women. They now had homes of their own and children of their own.

Unlike Willa, who had neither of those things. Instead, she laid her head on the pillow of professional success each night.

During the first few years of her acting career, coming home had been like attending a non-ending parade. There were special dinners in her honor, small speeches and long autograph lines at the local library, and even a tiny collection of memorabilia in her honor sold at one of the side booths in the General Store. Coming home with her twenty-eighth birthday looming and her acting career in its twilight hours was a different story. She would have preferred to slink through some sort of private, back entrance gate. One that led straight to her parents' home, safe from the inquisitive townspeople who couldn't wait for the latest tidbit of news about their local celebrity.

Then again, perhaps wearing her newest navy and purple travel gown and one-of-a-kind hats wasn't the best way to achieve anonymity. The moment Willa stepped off the train, she was thronged.

"Lord 'ave mercy, you're a sight for sore eyes!" Flash Billings, the local postman, made a wobbly dash in her direction. He smelled of cigar smoke and eggnog and didn't look a day older than a hundred and two with his nearly knee-length white beard. "I jes' delivered a letter to your Mum. She didn't say nothin' about you comin' home for th' holidays."

A pang of guilt rattled its way across Willa's conscience. She hadn't written home in awhile.

"They don't know," she admitted, hugging him back. "It was…" A bit last minute, even for her. "Supposed to be a surprise," she finished a trifle lamely, adoring the old familiar grain of his work jacket against her cheek. It smelled like the tobacco he stuffed into his nightly pipe. He was closer to seventy-two than a hundred and two, but he liked to keep his age a secret since he posed as the town's Santa every year, preferring the children to believe he was much older.

"Willa Murray!" Bea Ashburn squealed, edging her way in front of a pair of shop keepers who were waiting to greet her. "How dare you show up looking like a queen and catching me in my old shopping togs. That's rather unfair of you!" The moment Flash finished hugging her, Bea leaned in to press a cool, November kiss on her cheek. Her arms were too full of packages for a proper embrace.

"My apologies, love." Willa resisted the urge to roll her eyes. Bea, one of her closest childhood friends, didn't own anything old or anything that even minimally qualified as a "tog." Every item of clothing in her extensive wardrobe was tailor made by the best seamstresses in the state. Her goldenrod silk walking gown and oversized lacy bonnet were no exceptions. Not a stitch, ribbon, or strand of hair was out of place. Even in the light breeze, her glossy blonde ringlets seemed to bounce against her high cheek-bones in perfect unison.

A distance had sprung between them over the years, the kind born of spending months apart in lives traveling in opposite directions. Willa had chosen a career over having a family, while Bea had chosen a family over a career…in a manner of speaking. A live-in nanny was helping raise her twin six-year-old daughters, while she reined as the town princess in the highest social circles.

A position Willa used to hold. Back when she was a citizen of Pinetop. An insider. Which she no longer was.

The excited babble of her impromptu welcoming party dimmed as a tall, broad-shouldered man standing across the crowded train platform caught her eye. She didn't recognize him, which was odd since she knew almost everyone in town. His sun-kissed bronze features and black unbuttoned sack coat, which revealed a daring red and black plaid waistcoat, seemed a little out of place among the more sedately dressed townsfolk. However, no one was giving him any undue attention. He lounged against an extinguished light pole, arms folded, nodding and greeting an occasional passerby. They tipped their hats in return as they hurried past.

Like the cluster of people gathered around her, it appeared he'd paused to witness her arrival, though he obviously preferred doing it from a distance.

She didn't realize she was staring until he turned his head to ensnare her gaze. It was a slow, lazy movement that her instincts screamed was deliberate and calculated. Not a big surprise. She was accustomed to being flirted with by handsome and mysterious men. However, she wasn't prepared for the glint of taunting humor when his dark gaze clashed with hers. It reminded her way too much of a certain cocky, eight-year-old braggart from grammar school who'd been the bane of her existence once upon a time.

Angel Castellano.

He'd sworn to her entire circle of classy, well-dressed friends that he was going to marry her someday. To her distress, they'd laughed the proud little urchin to scorn.

She squinted at the man in the sunlight, but her brain simply couldn't connect the undernourished, poorly dressed son of a migrant worker she used to know with the much older, impeccably dressed, and highly polished gentleman smirking at her now.

No, it wasn't possible. It couldn't be him. It just couldn't!

Hope you enjoyed this excerpt from
ORNAMENTAL MATCH MAKER SERIES:
Angel Cookie Christmas
Available in eBook and paperback on Amazon + FREE to Kindle Unlimited subscribers!

Other books in this mini-series within a series include:
Star-Studded Christmas
Stolen Heart Valentine
Miracle for Christmas in July
Home for Christmas — *coming December, 2019*

Much love,
Jo

Sneak Preview: Hot-Tempered Hannah

U nlike his name suggested, there was nothing angelic about Gabriel Donovan. Quite the contrary. While most men were settled down with a wife and family by his ripe old age of twenty-six, he preferred the life of a bounty hunter, tracking and rounding up men who carried a price on their heads. He extracted money and information and taught an occasional lesson to particularly deserving scoundrels when circumstances warranted it.

Most people kept their distance from him, and he was okay with that. More than okay. Making friends wasn't part of the job, and he sincerely hoped he didn't run into anyone he knew at the Pink Swan tonight. Unlike the other patrons, he wasn't looking for entertainment to brighten the endless drag of mining activities in windy Headstone, Arizona. If any of the show girls from the makeshift stage at the front of the room bothered to approach him, they'd be wasting their time. He'd purposefully chosen the dim corner table for its solitude. All he wanted was a hot meal and his own thoughts for company.

"Why, if it isn't Gunslinger Gabe," a female voice cooed, sweet as honey and smoother than a calf's hide. She plopped a mug of watered down ale on the table, scrapping the metal cup in his direction. "I's beginning to worry you wasn't gonna show up for your Friday night supper."

"Evening, Layla." He hated her use of his nickname. Hated how the printed gazettes popping up across the West ensured he would never outride the cheeky title. It followed him from town to town like an infection. He hated it for one reason: None of his eight notorious years of quick draws and crack shots had been enough to save his partner during that fated summer night's raid.

It was a regret that weighed down his chest every second of every day like a ton of coal. It was a regret he would carry to his grave.

He nodded at the waitress who leaned one hand on the small round table with chipped black paint.

"Well, what's it going to be this time, cowboy?" Her dark eyes snapped with a mixture of interest and impatience. "Bean stew? Mutton pie? As purty as your eyes are, I got other tables to wait on, you know."

The compliment never failed to disgust him. Along with his angelic name, he'd been told more times than he cared to count that he'd been gifted with innocent features. If he heard another word about his clear, lake-blue eyes that inspired trust, he would surely vomit.

"Surprise me." He hoped to change the subject. Both entrees sounded equally good to him. He was hungry enough to eat the pewter serving ware, if she didn't hurry up with his order.

Layla's movements were slow as sap rolling down the bark of a maple tree. "If it's a surprise you're looking for...." She swayed a step closer.

"Bring me both," he said quickly. "The stew and the pie. I haven't eaten since this morning."

"Fine." The single word was infused with a world of derisive disappointment. A few steps into her stormy retreat, she spun around. Anger rippled in waves across her heart-shaped face. "I know what you really want."

"You do?" The question grated out past his lips before he could recall the words. Sarcastic and challenging. It had been a rough day. The last thing he needed was a saloon wench to whip out her crystal ball and presume to know anything about his life. Or his longings. No one this side of the grave could fill the void in his heart.

"I sure do, cowboy." She was back in front of him before he could blink, her scarlet dress shimmering with her movements. "An' I can show you a real special time. Something you ain't never gonna find on no supper menu."

He didn't figure any good would come of trying to explain that his heart belonged to a ghost. Wracking his brain for a sensible way to end their conversation without offending her further, he stared drearily at his mug. There was no quickening of his breathing around any women these days. No increased thump of his heartbeat. Not like there had been with Hannah. His dead partner. Or Hot-Tempered Hannah, as she'd been known throughout the West.

Then again, maybe he wasn't completely dead yet on the inside. He felt a stirring in the sooty, blackened, charred recesses of his brain as his memories of her sprang back to life. Memories that refused to die.

His mind swiftly conjured up all five feet three inches of her boyishly slender frame stuffed in men's breeches along with the tumultuous swing of red hair she'd refused to pin up like a proper lady. Nor could he forget the taunting tilt of her head and the voice that turned from sweet to sassy in a heartbeat, a voice that had been silenced forever due to his failure to reach their rendezvous in time.

Lord help him, but he was finally feeling something alright — a sharp gushing hole of pain straight through the chest. He mechanically reached for his glass and downed the rest of his ale in one harsh gulp.

"Well, I'll be!" The waitress peered closer at him, at first with amazement then with growing irritation. "I've been around long enough to know when a body's pining for someone else."

What? Am I that transparent? His brows shot up and he stared back, thoroughly annoyed at her intrusive badgering.

Layla was the first to lower her eyes. "Guess I'll get back to work, since you're of no mind to chat." Her frustration raised her voice to a higher pitch. "I was jes' trying to be friendly, you unsociable cad. I'll try not to burn your pie or spill your soup, since that's all you be wanting." Her voice scorched his ears as she pivoted in a full circle and stormed in the direction of the kitchen.

He stared after her, wishing he could call her back but knowing his apology wouldn't make her feel any better. A woman scorned was a deadly thing indeed. He could only hope she didn't poison his supper.

He hunched his shoulders over his corner table and went back to reminiscing about his dead partner. Known as Hot-Tempered Hannah throughout Arizona, she'd stolen his heart with a single kiss then threatened to shoot him if he ever tried to steal another.

He had yet to get over her. Hadn't looked at another woman since. She was three months in the grave, and he was nowhere near moving on with his life.

Layla stomped back in his direction twice. Once to refill his mug and several minutes later to dump his tray on the table with such a clatter that a few droplets of stew spilled over the edge of the bowl.

"A man at one of the faro tables paid me to deliver you a message," she snapped. "He wants you to stick around 'til he's finished dealing. Says he needs to speak with you 'bout somethin' important."

The drowsy contentedness settling in Gabe's bones from the hot meal sharpened back to full awareness. He paused in the act of lifting a spoonful of stew to his mouth. "Which man?"

She pointed to the nearest gaming table. "Over there. The one dealing."

Technically, the man was shuffling, but he pushed back his Stetson an inch and deliberately nodded a greeting in response to their curious stares. Gabe didn't recognize him. They were dressed much the same, albeit Gabe hadn't bothered to remove his trench coat like the other man had.

His keen bounty hunter eyes zeroed in on the ridge of

concealed weapons beneath the man's vest. Most people wouldn't have noticed, but Gabe wasn't most people. He was well paid to notice everything around him. The things people wanted him to notice and the things they preferred he didn't.

Those same sensory nodes told him Layla was still present, though she was standing behind him not making a peep. His gaze remained fixed on his summoner. "Does this faro dealer have a name?"

She sniffed. "He didn't say, and I ain't takin' extra to find out. He's working a little too hard for my tastes to fit in, if you know what I mean."

Gabe knew exactly what she meant and was surprised enough at her perception to spare her a glance. He reached in his pocket, and she tensed. He slid an extra bill in her direction across the scratched up tabletop. Something told him she could use the money. "Thanks for passing on the gentleman's message."

The frown on her lacquered lips eased. "Maybe some time you and I can visit a little longer, gunslinger?" She batted her lashes at him.

He highly doubted it — ever. "Dinner tastes wonderful. I thank you for that as well." He returned his hand to his soup spoon and his attention to the faro dealer. Something told him he was about to receive a new bounty assignment.

Layla lingered a few moments longer but finally left him on a drawn-out sigh of resignation.

He ate quickly while observing the card game. In seconds, he determined the game was rigged. Unlike most tables where the odds generally leaned in the banker's favor, this table broke even every few rounds. The intervals were entirely too regular to be coincidental. If Gabe's suspicions were correct, the faro dealer wasn't making a penny. *Very odd.* He chewed his mutton pie more slowly, watching the man.

When the man looked up between rounds, he allowed their gazes to clash once more. A nod from him had a new faro dealer rushing forward to claim the oval table with its green baize covering. The man closed down his rigged game, tucked his crooked gaming box beneath his arm, and sauntered in Gabe's direction amidst the cries for higher stakes from the newest dealer on the floor.

Gabe took in the man's tousled brown hair, even stride, and confident air. His senses told him the man was on a mission but not out for blood. Nevertheless, he kept a hand on his holster as the man stopped beside his table.

"May I join you?" The thick northeastern accent tickled his curiosity further.

A Bostonian, if Gabe was a betting man. Which he wasn't where money was concerned. He dipped his head in agreement without breaking eye contact.

The man took a seat, cradling the card box between his hands on the table in front of him. He was far more at ease than most men tended to be in the presence of Gunslinger Gabe. His long fingers were scarred on one hand, puckered and mottled a permanent shade of salmon as if he'd held his hand in a fire a few moments too long.

"I need your help." His words were simple and quietly spoken, not the usual hard-nosed beginning to a proper bounty negotiation. His tone was missing the sharp bite of revenge or the frantic pace of a man in a hurry.

Gabe leaned forward. "Most reputable men introduce themselves."

A half-grin softened the man's features another degree as he signaled Layla. "Most reputable men are fools. I'd much rather start a conversation by wetting my whistle."

Gabe's hand tightened on his holster. "And I'd rather start with a name."

The man shrugged. "Have it your way, gunslinger, but I'll have more to say if I wet my tongue first."

"I prefer to know who I'm drinking with."

"Fair enough." The man's grin widened as if he was pleased with what he was hearing. "I run my faro table under the name of Sharp Masterson."

"And your real name is?"

"Must you ask so many questions, gunslinger?"

"Most men prefer to keep me talking."

The man laughed aloud this time and reached for the drink Layla offered. Taking a sip, he eyed Gabe over the rim. "Colt Branson, since you insist on knowing."

Gabe shook his head. "Not ringing a bell. Don't suppose you go by any other handles?"

"Nope. I keep a low profile, but the second name I gave you is real enough."

The man's direct manner impressed Gabe as honest. It wasn't accompanied by the usual twitching and glancing away of a person with something to hide.

"I'm listening." Anxious to finish filling the clawing hole in his belly, he resumed eating his mutton pie with gusto. The sooner he finished eating, the sooner he could get moving again. He'd made many enemies in his line of business. As a rule, he never stayed too long in any one town.

Colt held his gaze with unwavering intensity. "As I said before, I need your help. More precisely, The Boomtown Mail Order Brides Company needs your help."

Boomtown what? Gabe waited a few heartbeats before attempting to swallow the bite of pie in his mouth. As it was, he had to choke it down and cough to clear his throat. If he had any laughter left in his soul, he would have laughed. "Clearly you're confused about what line of business I'm in, Mr. Branson."

The man waved his hand carelessly. "You can drop the mister. Just call me Colt. And you're exactly the kind of man I need for this job."

Gabe was only half listening as he finished up his last bite of pie and nursed the remaining swig or two of his ale. He swirled it around the bottom of his glass before taking a sip.

"We've lost contact with one of our brides-to-be."

Your problem. Not mine. Gabe raised his brows, incredulous that Colt had singled him out to share his sorry tale. Rescuing damsels in distress was a skill he simply didn't possess. Hot-Tempered Hannah was proof enough of that. A fresh splinter of pain ricocheted through his chest. He emptied his mug, hardly realizing he'd pressed a palm to his heart where his ache was the worse.

Colt's gaze followed his hand. "You and I both know the West isn't a safe place for young, marriageable women. Why so many of them flock to fill the ever-growing pile of mail order bride applications is thoroughly beyond me. Even the toughest among them don't always survive. Better to stay in more civilized cities back East."

Gabe wished the man would hurry up and get to his point. *Even the toughest…don't always survive.* The conversation was treading dangerously close to Hannah's tragic demise, making his trigger finger itch something powerful.

Colt abruptly shoved aside his dealer box to lean closer. He lowered his voice, but it accentuated rather than lessened the fierceness of his words. "My own sister, may she rest in peace, was one of those eager mail order brides. I'll never know why she decided to become one. Probably speculate myself into an early grave. Maybe it was because she wasn't much use with a needle and thread. Or maybe it was because anytime I caught her in the kitchen, I tended to skip dinner that night. But she could ride a horse like a demon, and she could hold her own with a gun." He shook his head admiringly, then sobered. "In the end, gunslinger, neither of those things could save MaryAnne from the cruelty of the man she married."

"What happened?" Gabe both wanted to know and didn't want to know.

"Her late husband claimed it was a stagecoach robbery that went south." He balled his hands into fists on the tabletop. "Said they were in the wrong place at the wrong time, but that doesn't explain the fire or the—" He fiercely bit off whatever else he was about to say and took a deep breath. "The stage company was kind enough to send her remains home, so we could lay her to rest."

It was a tragic tale, yet Gabe found himself envying the man his closure. As for himself, he'd never received a body to bury, only the news that Hot-Tempered Hannah was dead. He bit down on the inside of his cheek. Hard. Enough to draw the coppery tang of blood across his tongue. "I'm sorry for your loss but with all due respect, I don't see how any of this applies to me." Harsh but true.

Colt's upper lip curled. "I don't believe that for a second. Don't tell me you've never asked your Maker for a do-over."

"A do-over?"

"A second chance."

Leave it alone, mister. Gabe's hand literally tingled with the itch to draw and fire. Colt Branson clearly had no idea what dangerous ground he was treading. "I have no idea what you're talking about."

"Of course, you do, and that's why you're going to help me find Heloise."

"Who?" Gabe choked back a snarl. Maybe the man

was a bit touched in the head. It was the only explanation for his foolish persistence in toying with a gunslinger.

"She's one of our mail order brides. We should have received her letter by now, notifying us of her safe arrival to Headstone; but there've been no letters. No mention of her among the other brides we placed in neighboring towns. Nothing. She just—" He snapped his fingers. "Up and vanished!" His skin beneath his tan had paled, and he sounded truly distraught.

Gabe scrubbed a hand down his jaw, wishing he could offer a ray of comfort to the troubled faro dealer, touched in the noggin' or not. "Mail runs slow in some parts of the country. Maybe you should give it more time."

"We require our brides to write their letters before they leave Boston. All each of them has to do when she reaches her destination is date it and mail it."

"So have a chat with the post master."

For the first time in their short conversation, Colt's mouth gave an ugly downward twist of irritation. "Come on, gunslinger. I arrived here a week ago. Tracking down that fellow was the first thing on my list, and I was prepared to rip out his toenails one by one if need be to jog his memory of her. Except the poor chap seems to have vanished as well. I asked around town about him, but they said he was involved in some sort of stage coach accident. They found remnants of the carriage and wheels strewn down the side of a cliff but no bodies."

So the hopeful bride was missing. Tough times. She could be anywhere. Holed up in the mountains or chained inside a brothel, her virtue a distant memory. Anger churned in Gabe's gut. Unfortunately, things like that happened on occasion in the wild West. Some women just weren't meant to travel to these dusty towns of lonely, lust-crazed, and sometimes desperate men. Not everyone could hold their own or go out guns a-blazing like Hot-Tempered Hannah had.

Colt's missing Heloise was dead or as good as dead. Gabe wasn't a doomsday kind of guy; he was just facing the facts. Why then did questions start to bubble up his throat about the unfortunate woman?

"How long has she been missing, and what did she look like?" he blurted. Was she pretty enough to attract the attention of a madame? Had Colt bothered to scope out the brothels in the nearest towns?

He didn't know why he was asking. He certainly had no intention of helping Colt and his mail order bride company. Not for any price. He was too afraid of what he might find on the other end. The carnage. And death.

Too afraid of failing to save another woman.

Colt's shoulders relaxed a fraction at the barrage of questions, though his forearms remained resting on the edge of the table. The music in the background transitioned from a swinging ballad to something rowdier. The room grew louder. And hotter. And more suffocating.

Gabe could only pray he and Colt were about finished with their miserable discussion. Lord help him, he needed some fresh air.

"The last time any of us saw Heloise was two months ago when she boarded her train. She was wearing a simple brown taffeta gown." Colt's face settled into another half-grin. "When she first came to us, she had the kind of red hair no comb can tame, though the Boom-town matrons on our staff tried their best. They couldn't tame her mouth either. Or erase the bruises way down deep in her eyes. Impressed me as one of those wild little fillies who's seen things she didn't care to talk about. Our other brides-to-be tried to befriend her, but she mostly kept to herself. Kind of haunted like. Not that she would have fit in with them anyway." He gave a long, drown-out sigh of regret. "Reminded me of my sister, MaryAnne. She wasn't soft or gently spoken. Not skilled in any womanly arts that I could tell. She didn't look all that comfortable in a dress either, come to think of it. But she was full of fire no scoundrel has the right to put out before her time."

Colt's description of the young woman made Gabe swallow hard. Heloise sounded like Hot-Tempered Hannah all over again. A free spirit. An untamed heart with a thirst for adventure. And deader than dead if she'd already been missing for two full months.

There was no way Colt Branson could possibly know every one of his words sank into his listener like a gunshot. By the time the faro dealer was through describing his missing bride-to-be, it was all Gabe could do to remain sitting upright in his chair. His chest and torso were so riddled with emotional holes, he wouldn't have been the least shocked to feel the drip of blood on the hands he had fisted on his thighs.

Another woman was dead. It was an old, tired tale. Hell simply wasn't big enough for all the scum-eating rene-gades crawling the landscape these days. The gold-hungry, devil-may-care, barely human creatures who lived for little more than the next thrill. They were affection-starved and utterly depraved. Men who couldn't remember what it was like to be in the presence of a real lady. Men who wouldn't hesitate to take advantage of one, given half a chance.

"I'm sorry. I can't help you." Colt could shower his ears with all the piteous pleas in the world, but it wouldn't bring the missing bride one step closer to being found. It would be easier to locate a five-leaf clover in a field of December snow. Heloise was gone. The sooner Colt accepted the fact, the better.

"Can't or won't?" Colt snarled, gripping the edges of the table with both hands.

"Can't. Won't. Does it matter? She's gone." Gabe pushed away from the table and stood, desperate for a mouthful of fresh air before his lungs exploded.

"Is that what you want to believe?" Colt stood as well. "Because you buried your partner's body like I buried my sister's?"

How in tarnation did Colt know so much about his past when they'd never met before tonight? "Watch yourself, Sharp." Gabe's hand slid to his gun holster again. Hannah had been burnt alive; there had been nothing left to bury. Something told him Colt knew this, too.

"Did you?" Colt pressed. "Because if you did, then I'm wasting my breath by telling you the Boomtown Mail Order Brides Company received a ransom note for Heloise."

Meaning the poor woman might still be alive after all. And probably wishing she was dead...

"How much?" Gabe gritted through his teeth, making an inhuman effort to keep his voice down.

"Two grand."

It was a fortune. More than most lawmen made in a year and bigger than any other single bounty Gabe had earned. "Why so much?"

"Her abductor didn't say, but he seemed awfully concerned about listing every known name in the ransom note that Heloise might have ever used. Hester. Holly." He paused, dipping his head to peer beneath Gabe's Stetson. "Hannah."

For a moment, Gabe couldn't hear past the buzzing in his head. Hester and Holly were among the many aliases Hot-Tempered Hannah had used on their string of joint assignments as bounty hunters.

"Oh, and here's the sketch another one of our mail order brides made of Heloise the night before she traveled West to meet her intended groom." Colt reached inside his vest and withdrew a charcoal portrait. He held it out.

Gabe reached for the small square of canvas and his insides went numb. He took a stumbling step towards the table and sank back into his seat. A coldness like he'd never known before spread through his chest. The sketch wasn't a perfect likeness, but it was close enough. There was no mistaking the challenging tilt of the woman's face or the determined set to her chin.

It was Hannah or someone who resembled her enough to pass as her twin, which made no sense. Hannah had never mentioned a sister. She'd never mentioned having family at all, for that matter.

The sketch slid from his nerveless fingers to the table. He slowly leaned forward on his elbows to grip his head in both hands. He closed his eyes, uncaring that his movements sent his Stetson tumbling to the floor. He fisted his hair roots until the tearing pressure on his skull rivaled the screaming questions in his brain.

There was another possibility — one that filled him with frantic joy and raging agony — that, by some miracle, Hannah was alive.

If it were true, it could only mean one thing. She'd faked her death. But why? Had she done it to double-cross him and take their final bounty purse for herself? Was it possible the woman he'd loved with every ounce of his life had secretly despised him in return? So much so that she'd been that desperate to get rid of him?

Gabe's heart felt like it was festering with a thousand blisters. The worst part about the possibility that Hannah was still alive was the fact she was trying to marry another man.

He didn't know how long he sat there. It could have been minutes or hours before the red-hot lava of anger finally burst through his numbness. Heat shot through his bloodstream and gave him the strength to lower his hands and meet Colt's concerned gaze. He needed answers. No, he desperately craved them, and there was only one way to get them. "I'm going to find her."

He would track her down, haul her double-crossing hide back to Headstone, and demand answers to every question scorching the walls of his soul. She owed him that at least.

"I know you will." Colt produced a folded parchment and slid it across the table in his direction. "Here's our contract. We'll cover your travel expenses, and there will be a sizable reward when you return her to us. Not anywhere near as big as the ransom note but enough to make it worth your while."

Gabe wasn't taking anyone's money. Not for this job. Finding Hannah was strictly personal. He started to crumple the contract, but Colt's eyelids narrowed to warning slits.

"You'll not lay eyes on the ransom note until you sign my contract."

The maniacal thought ran through Gabe's head that he could shoot Colt's knees out from under him and torture him into giving him what he wanted, but Colt didn't exactly impress him as a man who would buckle quickly or easily under pressure. And Gabe didn't have time to quibble. Heloise had already been missing two months. The clock was ticking.

When Colt handed him a pen, he scrawled a hasty signature. "Tell me everything you know."

"I will as soon as you raise your right hand and repeat your oath of allegiance to the Gallant Rescue Society."

Gallant who? Never mind. It didn't matter. Gabe's insides churned with determination as he recited the oath, hardly registering the words coming from his mouth. "I hereby solemnly pledge my gun and my honor to the Gallant Rescue Society...so help me God."

Like a stallion pawing at the ground, he was frothing at the mouth to break into a gallop on his mission. The only thing in the world that mattered anymore was finding Hannah. He'd start his search in the Yellow Diamond Mine on the outskirts of Headstone. It was where she'd supposedly burnt to death during a premature dynamite explosion in an underground tunnel. A place of business he swore he'd never return to. The home of a gang of squatters who wanted him dead.

Hope you enjoyed this excerpt from
THE MAIL ORDER BRIDES RESCUE SERIES:
Hot-Tempered Hannah
Available in eBook and paperback on Amazon + FREE to Kindle Unlimited subscribers!
Other books in this series include:
Cold-Feet Callie
Fiery Felicity
Misunderstood Meg
Dare-Devil Daisy
Outrageous Olivia
Jinglebell Jane — *coming December, 2019*

Much love,
Jo

Read More Jo

I write — a lot! And I'm currently writing these series:

- **Mail Order Bride Rescue Series** — *a mad dash of gallant rescuers in a sweet series to fetch all the mail order brides from the mayhem that befalls them on their journey West!*
- **Her Billionaire Series** — *a sweet contemporary romantic rivalry between two mega corporate dynasties in the Alaskan Gulf! You can expect several more titles in this series in 2020!*
- **Lost Colony Series** — *a pre-colonial epic saga about the Lost Colonists of Roanoke Island. In the first book, a working class girl poses as a male clerk to gain passage on a ship bound for the New World. She encounters a deadly conspiracy, pirates, and a dreamy Native chief who offers his protection for a price. This finale to this series will release just in time for Thanksgiving, 2019.*
- **Ornamental Match Maker Series** — *a fun and cozy, super sweet holiday multi-author series!*
- **Other Multi-Author Series** — Disaster City Search & Rescue Series, The Pinkerton Matchmaker, and the Holliday Islands Resort, among others. More new titles coming every month!

You can find out more about each series by visiting my
Amazon Author Page:
amazon.com/author/jografford

Or by liking me on Bookbub:
https://www.bookbub.com/authors/jo-grafford

Or by joining my Cuppa Jo Reader Group to chat books,
celebrate new releases, participate in games and giveaways,
plan meet-ups at book-lover conferences, and more at:
https://www.facebook.com/groups/CuppaJoReaders

One other super special place I like to hang out online is
the Heroes and Hunks Reader Group at:
https://www.facebook.com/groups/HeroesandHunks/

Happy reading! — Jo

Made in the USA
Middletown, DE
15 November 2019

78740088R00080